KLAYTON'S TREASURE 3

THEA

Published by Urban Chapters Publications
www.urbanchapterspublications.com

Contains explicit languages and adult themes
suitable for ages 16+

WHERE WE LEFT OFF ....

Klayton

I had gotten Treasure discharged and settled in the house no one other than my family knew about. I made sure Giovanni and Hope both were aware of where I lived out of courtesy because that was their youngest child. Other than that, I was trying to lay low until I could get to the bottom of where this fuck nigga, Kamar, was at. He clearly wanted smoke, but he wasn't prepared to bring that heat in my direction. I picked my daughter, Danielle, up from Ro and Trayce because they had been watching her, and I needed to spend more time with my own child. Danielle had been helping me take care of Treasure and declared herself Treasure's nurse. She was tired, so I put her down to take a nap, and now I was trying to attend to Treasure. I had hired an assistant named Brandy that was due to come over tomorrow to start helping me out. I wanted nothing more than to cupcake with Treasure and Danielle, but I couldn't relax until I killed Kamar.

"Klayton, bae. Can you bring me some juice, please?" Treasure whined in the intercom that I had installed in the house. Anytime she needed something, I had it on strict orders that she was not supposed to get up and get it herself. I would get it for her and if I wasn't home,

I hired a bitch named Brandy that came highly recommended as an assistant. All she had to do was be at Treasure's beck and call whenever I wasn't home.

"I'm coming, bae."

I could have had maids attend to my every need since I came from generational wealth, but I had always been a real simple nigga. Fuck did I need five Maybachs, a butler and a maid for? See, that was how niggas got caught up and went broke, trying to keep up with the Joneses. I had more than enough money for ten different lifetimes, but I had never been a real flashy nigga. Now, Treasure could get all of my coins so she could match my fly, but she didn't even strike me as the gold-digging type.

I went and got some orange juice, cheese and crackers and put them on a tray for Treasure to snack on. She was able to eat solid foods now, and her well-being was my main concern. The only thing that would trump that was putting a bullet in that fuck nigga Kamar's dome. I grabbed the snacks and brought them up for Treasure to enjoy.

"Thanks, bae. Can you pass me my iPhone XR?" Treasure gave me a sloppy kiss, and I enjoyed every second of it. It felt good knowing that Treasure was a fighter and she was going to push through.

Without even giving it a second thought, I passed Treasure her cell phone. She opened it and was focused on whatever she was looking at on her phone screen. Whatever it was, it had her visibly upset because her hands started trembling and shaking.

"Treasure, what is wrong?" I asked, obviously confused.

"Get away from me, you fucking liar! I thought you loved me." Treasure started weeping. It sounded like her dog fucking died, but I had no idea what I did wrong.

"I am not a liar. Tell me what is wrong so I can fix it, bae," I pleaded. Her tears had a nigga ready to get on bended knee and kiss her feet even though I had no idea what I did wrong.

"Fix this, you lying, cheating scumbag. Don't even think about lying to me because the time stamp on the picture is from when I was in a coma. I almost died for you, Klayton, and this is how you fucking repay me? By getting your dick sucked in a fucking club? How could you cheat on me?" Treasure cried.

My face turned as pale as Casper the fucking ghost when I realized that I was busted. Someone must have taken a picture of me getting my dick sucked and sent it to Treasure. I could have sworn there was no one in the fucking bathroom when that happened. How the hell did I get caught slipping in such a major way?

"Listen, Treasure—"

"Get the fuck out of our house, Klayton! I wish I never met you, and I fucking hate you! I am so glad I never gave you my virginity!" Treasure screamed, and my heart broke into pieces. In my eyes, Treasure was still a virgin since the only time that she had sexual intercourse, she was raped by that fuck nigga, Blach.

"How you gon' kick a nigga out of his own house, Treasure? I know I fucked up, but—"

I didn't even get to finish the sentence before Treasure pulled a gun out of the drawer next to her. She took off the silencer and pointed the gun at me without even blinking an eye. Her face was void of expression, and I knew I had created a monster at that point. She was really going to kill me over a misunderstanding. Granted, I fucked up, but I wanted to make things right. I needed another chance.

"Get out, Klayton. I never should have given you the chance to break my heart. After everything that I have been through, Klayton. Your betrayal hurts me more than anything Blach ever did!" Treasure sobbed, and her words cut me like a sword that went straight to my heart. I knew I was wrong, but did she really have to go there with a nigga?

"Treasure, all that bitch did was top me off with some dome. I was missing you and heartbroken."

"Hoes like you never fucking change, Klayton. Luca was right about you breaking my heart. And I chose you over my brother, but for what? You proved my brother was right. You were so heartbroken that you let the next bitch suck on what was supposed to be mine. I know that we never had sex, but I was dumb. I was stupid to think a nigga like you, who could have any woman that he wants, would wait for me. Get out, Klayton. If I could go anywhere, I would and since I can't, that means you got to go. Now!" Treasure screamed.

I needed to get through to her. I couldn't leave her here alone, especially with my daughter here. She wasn't in the position to care of Danielle by herself.

"The hell I am getting out of my own house, bitch! My daughter and I live here, too!" I was wrong two ways from Sunday, but I was hurt that Treasure would sit there and compare me to that fuck nigga, Blach, that raped her.

"Leave Danielle here. I will make sure she is okay. You have ten seconds to leave before your child becomes fatherless!" Treasure yelled.

Meanwhile, throughout this altercation, neither of us noticed that Danielle woke up from her nap and walked into the room. Things would have gone completely different if we knew Danielle was in the room. Emotions were riding high, and neither of us were thinking clearly. Before I could blink an eye, Treasure pressed the trigger and the gun went off.

Pow! Pow!

My heart broke when I realized my daughter's lifeless body was on the ground next to mine. I looked at Treasure despondently.

"I can't believe you would do me like that, you evil, heartless bitch."

1

KLAYTON

"Klayton, I am so sorry! I didn't mean to shoot Danielle!" Treasure yelled.

The sound of Treasure's voice irritated me, and it was all I could do to not body her ass. Nothing breaks your heart more than your child being shot and not knowing if she was going to make it. Time felt like it stopped, and I instinctively got into protective daddy mode. I went to pick up Danielle's limp body and as soon as I picked her up, she opened her eyes.

"Daddy! Daddy, I'm scared!" Danielle cried. I instantly wished I could trade places with her because no parent should have to bury their child.

"Baby, are you ok?" I started checking her body and saw no blood anywhere. She must have passed out from the sound of the gun going off. There was a nice sized hole in the wall due to the bullet, but that was the last thing that was on my mind. I was dead set on getting her checked out at the hospital just to be sure that my daughter was ok.

"Daddy, I'm scared."

Danielle was clinging to my body. She wouldn't have to worry about a damn thing as long as there was breath in my damn body. I quickly glanced at Treasure, and she looked relieved that Danielle was talking, but I wasn't fucking with her off rip. She knew that my daughter was in the house and granted she was supposed to have been taking a nap, but she shouldn't have been acting so careless with a damn gun in her hand. I understood that Treasure was upset about the text message she got, but she was dead ass wrong and it could have cost my daughter her life.

"Everything is going to be ok, Danielle. Daddy will protect you. Let me go get you a jacket and we can go get you checked out at the emergency room." I sprang into action and carried my daughter into her room to get her a sweater. I also grabbed a change of clothes and some toys to keep her occupied while we were at the hospital. I still needed to deal with Treasure, but that would have to take a backseat until I made sure my daughter was good. I grabbed my phone and dialed Trayce's number.

"Yo', what's up, bruh?" Trayce answered. It sounded like the nigga was balls deep inside of Ro's pussy, but it was time to break that fuck fest up.

"Meet me at Little Company of Mary's emergency room now. Danielle got hurt!" I yelled and then hung up the phone.

I didn't have time to stay on the phone and listen to Trayce ask questions when I knew he would meet my ass there. I purposely didn't give him too many details because I needed to hurry up and get to the hospital. Thankfully, my daughter appeared to be ok but because her body hit the ground, I wasn't sure if there was a risk of a concussion.

I ran to my Range Rover and placed Danielle in her booster seat. I hopped in the driver's seat only to see Treasure sitting in the passenger seat. This bitch was lucky I didn't have time to argue with her ass. I stared at her ass for a second before I started the engine and started driving. The tension was thick as hell between us while I drove to the hospital. I felt Treasure staring at me and if she knew what was better for her, she would look in the other direction. I have no words for her and as far as I was concerned, our relationship was over.

"Listen, Klayton I—"

"Shut the fuck up, Treasure! You could have killed my fucking daughter. I will deal with your stupid ass later, ok?" I exploded. Now was not the time or the place and if she said anything else, I was likely to pull over and slap her ass one good time.

"Klayton, I'm sorry! I didn't mean to."

I quickly pulled the car over to the side of the road. Treasure thought I was playing with her ass today, but I had something for her. "Do you have your phone with you?" I interrupted Treasure.

She gave me a quizzical stare and responded. "Yes."

"Let me see it for a second." I held my hand out and she gave it to me. I quickly forwarded the text message from her phone to mine and then unlocked the passenger door.

"Klayton, what are you doing?" Treasure asked.

I didn't respond to her question. Instead, I got out of the car, walked over to her side of the car and opened her door. I reached over and unbuckled Treasure's seat belt and then picked her ass up. This bitch was going to have to get the fuck out of my car and get herself a fucking Uber. The love that I have for Treasure was quickly turning to hate, and what she did was unforgivable.

"Call your ass an Uber, hoe. I will have your things delivered to Luca's house in the next couple of days." I dropped her ass on the ground, and she got pissed off. She had no room to be mad when she was the reason that we were in this situation now.

"How the fuck are you going to leave me on the side of the fucking road, Klayton? You are a fuck boy just like my brother said you were. I know that I messed up, but you won't even let me try to make things right. I just want to be sure that Danielle is going to be ok." Treasure was pissed and had tried to kick me, but she missed. Reckless Klayton was starting to come back and I knew that wasn't good for either of us because I was liable to kill Treasure.

I quickly ran to the driver's side of the car and got in. I locked the doors from the inside so she couldn't get back in the car, then sped off, leaving Treasure stranded on the side of the fucking road. You guys might be upset at me for abandoning Treasure on the side of the road, but she was heartless trying to kick me out of my own house and waving a gun around carelessly, almost causing my daughter to die. Thankfully, it looked like my daughter had just gotten scared by the sound of the gun, but I wanted to be sure there was no damage done to her. Treasure could call her ass an Uber and get to Luca's house. Right now, she didn't deserve to breathe the same air as Danielle or go with us to the hospital.

My phone continued going off, and I ignored it. I was focused on driving to the hospital and made it there ten minutes later. I saw Trayce, Ro and my nephew, Matthew, was asleep on Trayce's shoulder.

"Yo', what happened?" Trayce asked.

I didn't even have the energy to answer Trayce's question. My daughter is my first priority and I was going to raise hell until she got treated. I walked past them to the receptionist desk and started yelling.

"My daughter needs medical attention! She needs to get checked out because she passed out after a gunshot went off in my house!"

"I need you to fill out this paperwork and someone will be with you as soon as possible," the receptionist whispered in a monotone voice. This bitch was lucky I had my daughter in my hand.

Trayce was next to me, and he started cutting up. Trayce choked this hoe up and she looked like that hoe from BAP. "Listen, my niece is hurt, and she needs to be seen NOW! Fuck this fucking paperwork. We will be paying out of fucking pocket. Get the next available doctor to see her and get Danielle a room now."

She obviously knew better than to try to challenge us too much. As soon as Trayce put her ass down, she summoned us to follow her to a private room. "Dr. Wentworth will be with you guys shortly."

"Daddy, I'm scared!" Danielle cried and I felt like the worst kind of father. I was supposed to protect my child and keep her out of harm's way, and I failed her. If this was what falling in love was like, then love was for the birds. I would go back to being reckless Klayton fucking with birds to get my dick wet.

"Daddy is sorry he didn't protect you. I love you, Danielle. Everything is going to be ok," I whispered as tears slid down my face.

I knew that Trayce and Ro wanted to ask me what the hell happened, but I was saved by the doctor coming into the room.

"Hello, what is this beautiful little girl's name? I am, Dr. Wentworth and I will be her doctor. Can you give me an idea about what brings you in to see me today?" He asked.

I started giving him the details of what happened earlier and felt sick by the time I was done talking.

"First, I am going to run some MRI and CAT scans to make sure everything checks out with Danielle. I want to be sure that she didn't suffer from any head injuries from the fall. I am also afraid that I am going to have to call CPS because I am a mandated reporter. Whenever there is suspected child abuse or neglect involved, I have to report it or risk losing my license—"

"What the fuck? I would never let anyone put my daughter in any fucking danger!" I was brought down to my knees hearing that CPS might take my child away from me over something I couldn't fucking control. I suddenly wished I let Treasure come with me to the hospital, so I could choke the living shit out of her ass for putting me in this predicament.

"I am sorry, Mr. Jackson, but this is standard protocol. Now if you don't mind, I have the attendant ready to take Danielle down to the imaging room, and I need to contact CPS to come down here and start the investigation." Dr. Wentworth looked apologetic. I didn't give a fuck about this nigga's job. I was not about to have my daughter go in the fucking system because that would break me. I tried to get close enough to choke his ass, but Trayce stepped his big ass in between us.

"Klayton, let them do their investigation. You don't want to do something that you end up regretting and lose Danielle permanently. I know what happened wasn't your fault, but you need to stay strong for Danielle right now."

The doctor took that opportunity to make his exit from the hospital room. I walked over to Danielle's side and gave her a kiss on the cheek. "Daddy loves you, baby girl."

The attendant named Carlos came to take my daughter away, and I slumped into the nearest chair. I looked at Trayce and Ro in despair.

"What am I going to do if I lose Danielle? That little girl is my light and my reason to breathe—"

"We are only going to speak positive things into existence, Klayton. CPS will see that this was an accident and let you take your daughter home," Ro tried reassuring me, but I wasn't convinced.

Deep down, I just knew they were going to put Danielle in the system. I felt like I was on the brink of insanity, and I was about to lose my fucking mind. Trayce wrapped me up in a brotherly hug and didn't say anything to me.

"You know Ro and I are going to be here for you. We are going to do everything we can to keep your daughter out of the system. Danielle is not going into the system," Trayce repeated Ro's sentiments.

"I hope you are right, but I have a feeling that I might be screwed."

2

TREASURE

I could not believe Klayton flipped the script on me and left me on the side of the road. I get that I messed up and Danielle could have been seriously hurt, but it looked like she was going to be ok. What was the big deal? I knew all about Klayton having screws loose, but he never showed that reckless side to me until now. I called for an Uber and luckily, one arrived quickly. It was freezing cold under thirty degrees in Southern California and yes, that is cold to us out here on the West Coast. I was embarrassed because the second Luca saw me, he was going to go *'I told you so'* about me dating Klayton.

"Would you like any water or gum?" Ronaldo, my Uber driver, asked me.

"No, thank you," I whispered quietly.

Thankfully, he took the hint that I wanted to stay to myself and remained quiet for the rest of the drive. Part of me wanted to go to the hospital and see how Danielle was doing, but Klayton and I definitely needed time apart right now. I would call and see if there were any updates on Danielle's condition later on.

I made it home twenty minutes later and was alarmed at how

quiet it was at home. I prayed Luca was at work, and I wouldn't have to hear his shit, but luck really wasn't on my side.

"What are you doing here, Treasure? Aren't you supposed to be out there with your nigga, Klayton?" Luca asked bitterly.

"We broke up, Luca. Leave me alone," I whispered and headed towards my room. Unfortunately, Luca felt like following me with his miserable ass.

"Naw, why would you break up with his ass now? Did he fucking put his hands on you? I will kill his ass—"

"Shut up, Luca! He didn't put his hands on me, so leave me alone!" I screamed. My parents walked out and stared at us.

"Why are you guys arguing? Treasure, I thought you were at Klayton's house?" My mom looked confused.

"Nothing. Can you guys please stop asking me about Klayton, dammit? I just need some time to be by myself!" I stomped off and tears were sliding down my cheek.

I didn't want my parents to see me breaking down. Was this what it was like to have a broken heart? If so, love needed to stay the hell away from me and I would be content with Genesis and myself.

I made it to my room but not before my mom caught up to me. "Listen, chile. I know heartbreak when I hear it, and I know my daughter needs me right now. We are going to talk, honey. I thought things were good with you and Klayton?"

I made sure to lock the door after my mom walked inside of the room. "Mom, I don't even want to go into details. I should have listened to Luca when he told me Klayton wasn't shit. That man is incapable of love."

"Treasure, you are wrong. That man loves you more than life itself. When you were in that coma, he was there visiting you every day, and he cried for you. His words and his actions are of a man that is in love."

"Mom, he cheated on me while I was in a fucking coma. Someone sent me a text message showing some bitch giving him head. Look at this, mom." I grabbed my phone and pulled the text message up on my phone. I shoved the phone in my mother's face and tears slid down my face.

While I was fighting for my life in a coma that was due to his street shit, he was out there letting bitches top his ass off. I thought Klayton loved me, but he is incapable of loving anyone other than himself.

"Who sent you this? Come here, baby." My mom reached out for me, and I fell into her arms and started sobbing.

Klayton was my first true love and my first and only heartbreak. I would never open myself up to another man the way I did with Klayton. All I have known in my twenty-one years of life is heartbreak and betrayal. I should have known things wouldn't work out with Klayton.

"I don't know. It is some nigga with a New York area code. Let me call this number." I dialed the number and some nigga answered the phone.

"Treasure, I see you got the message that I sent you. That nigga Klayton you are fucking with ain't shit, and I want you to let him know Kamar is coming for him."

Who the fuck is Kamar and what the fuck does he want? "Listen, I don't know you. How the hell did you get my phone number?"

"My name is Kamar Lewis, and I run shit all along the east coast. Soon, you might be calling me zaddy when I play with that pretty pink pussy of yours."

My mom grabbed the phone from me and hung up on him. "Treasure, this has to be the nigga that is coming for Klayton. Let me school you on the game, honey. We don't even know if that picture he has is real or photoshopped. You need to give Klayton a chance to explain himself and give his side of the story. Trust me, I know how shit goes in the streets. Do not judge until you got the full story," My mom advised me.

I was feeling confused. I really wanted to believe that picture was photoshopped or Klayton had a reasonable explanation for it, but I knew that deep down that bitch sucked on what was supposed to be mine. "Mom, I didn't tell you the entire story. Klayton basically admitted that he fucked up and then I lost it."

"How did you lose it, chile? There is no way Klayton would have let you come back here without raising some hell unless you did something. I am surprised that nigga isn't here kicking the damn door down after your ass."

"I grabbed a gun and threatened to shoot him. I wasn't really going to kill him, but shit got out of hand. I didn't know Danielle woke up from her nap and walked in the room and—"

"Treasure, do not tell me you shot his daughter!" My mom yelled and her hands were visibly shaking.

"Well, not really. The bullet missed and made a hole in the wall, but it almost hit her. Danielle fell to the ground, so Klayton is at the hospital now with her. I was going to go with him, but we got into it, I called an Uber and came home." I purposely made sure to not tell my mom that Klayton left me abandoned on the side of the road because that would make my parents hate him. Even with everything that we were going through now, I still have a soft spot for the nigga.

"Well, that explains why he hasn't come after you. Sweetie, he loves you, but his daughter could have died. You are going to have to give him time and space to cool off. What I do know is he is in love with you, so you need to give him time." My mom gives good advice, but what about my feelings? He got caught cheating, but my mom was more concerned about his feelings.

"Wait a minute. He cheated on me and you're worried about me giving him time?" I asked incredulously.

"Chile, his daughter could have died! That trumps him getting his dick sucked in a club. How would you have felt if it was Genesis that was placed in that situation?" My mom asked.

"I would kill Klayton," I admitted honestly. I understood why he was upset, but he didn't even give me the chance to apologize.

"That man is angry right now and he has every right to be, Treasure. The only thing I can say is to give him time and hopefully, he will come back around."

"I hate to sound selfish, but he was supposed to be loyal to me when I was in that fucking coma. He instigated all of this by getting his dick sucked and putting himself in this position. There never should have been anything for that Kamar nigga to send me. Ultimately, it is his fault this situation is happening," I insisted.

"You both are wrong, Treasure. Chile, you are still young-minded as hell. I could have understood you leaving him and calling one of us to come pick you up. Instead, you go off of your emotions and almost killed his daughter. That is almost unforgivable, but right now you are in your feelings, so I will let you have that. I will go make you some tea, and I want you to focus on resting. I know it sounds like I'm being hard on you, but I always will be, to be honest with you. That man is in a position that no parent should have to be in, and we need to pray that Danielle will be ok."

"Mom, I really didn't mean for that to happen. It was an accident." I broke down and started crying. Truthfully, I would never forgive myself if Danielle was seriously hurt. I should have reacted differently, but sometimes you don't know what you are going to do until you find yourself in a situation.

"Baby, I know, and Klayton will come around in time. What hospital is Danielle at?" My mom asked.

"Little Company of Mary. Will you call and get an update on Danielle Jackson's condition? I know if I go up there, Klayton probably has my ass banned from visiting." I felt horrible and I prayed that Danielle would be ok. I was just glad she wasn't actually hit by that damn bullet, or I would have never forgiven myself.

"I got you. Get some rest, and I will make that call. I'm going to keep Luca out of here, or I will beat the tar out of his ass myself. It seems like he wants everyone to be as miserable as he has been lately," my mom muttered to herself. She got up off of the bed and I grabbed her hand.

"Mom, I might go to a hotel for a few days just to get away from Luca. I don't know what is wrong with him, but I can't be here if he is acting an entire donkey. Maybe Genesis can come with me and I can get some time with her?" I suggested, and my mom looked at me.

"It isn't safe for you and Genesis to leave with what is going on with that Kamar nigga. Your dad and I just bought a house out here, and I'm working on furnishing it. You and Genesis will be coming with me. It will be habitable in the next day or so," my mom explained, and I was ecstatic. I had no idea my parents were moving back to LA. I needed them by my side more than ever right now.

"Are you serious? Why are you just saying something? That is amazing news!" I squealed. I needed some good news to hang on to and got just the news that I had needed.

"I wasn't planning on saying anything yet, but I would rather you come with me and your dad than go to a hotel. We still need to go back to New York, wrap things up there and put the house there up for sale. I love you, Treasure, and we will get through this as a family," My mom reassured me before she left me to my thoughts.

I definitely was planning to move into her new home because I could be closer to Genesis, and I needed some space from Luca. What if Klayton never forgave me for the accident? How would I be able to go on with my life knowing that a big part of me was missing?

3

LUCA

I didn't want to gloat, but I was happy that my sister was home where she belonged. My phone has been on do not disturb since Gigi left my ass. I thought she would come to her senses soon, but I missed her. I was lashing out on everyone else due to the pain I was feeling, but I didn't care. If I was miserable then everyone else around me was going to be miserable too. I had gotten the text message from a New York area code with a picture of Gigi sucking Klayton's dick. There were so many questions in my mind. How the hell did she know the nigga? I had looked at the time stamp and noticed the date was before Gigi and I hooked up. I had no reason to be mad because she didn't know about my history with Klayton until recently, but I was jealous. Why did that nigga have to have everything that I had? The fact of the matter was this shit happened while my sister was in a coma so maybe I finally would be able to reason with her about how he was no good for her ass.

"What the fuck is your problem, Luca?" My father roared and he got in my face. He was coming at me like he owned shit in this bitch. The last time I checked, I was the owner of this house.

"Yo' pops, get the fuck out of my face—" I didn't even get to finish what I was saying before he punched me in the face. I instantly grabbed my nose and it felt like it was broken.

"Man, what did you have to break my nose for, Pops? That was foul!" I was exaggerating a bit but hell, my father should have been on my side. I had just discovered Klayton had gotten over on my ass again, and he was coming at me like he was crazy.

"You will be alright, Luca. You are miserable and bringing everyone else down around you lately. Your mom and I just bought a house out here and soon you will be alone to sulk in your misery. You weren't raised to feel sorry for yourself."

"You are talking all of this cash money shit, but you were never here to raise me, nigga! I had to be the fucking man of the family. Do you understand how it feels living with the fact that I couldn't protect Treasure? I love Genesis with all of my heart, but she is a constant reminder of how I failed my sister." I grabbed a towel and held it to my nose. I probably needed to go to the hospital and get it taped up and shit, but I was going to tough this shit out.

"That is what all of this about? Your mom and I have been telling you that you need help, Luca, to deal with past issues. We love you, and Treasure never blamed you for anything that happened to her."

"She doesn't have to blame me when I know deep down that it was my fault. Then she goes with a fuck nigga that broke her heart, and I don't want her to have to go through more hardships. My sister should be able to sit pretty and enjoy the rest of her life, not feel pain, Dad." I poured my heart out. I know it seems like I don't care about my sister's feelings, but I care more than anyone knows. I have a hard time expressing myself at times. It was a hard pill to swallow watching your sister fall in love with your arch nemesis. Klayton and I will never be friends, mark my words.

"You don't even know the details of what happened, and you are jumping to conclusions about Klayton. Let me tell you something. The entire time Treasure was in the hospital, he was up there checking on her almost every day. Now where the fuck were you? Don't throw stones when your shit is dirty as well, Luca."

"Are you trying to insinuate that I don't love my sister? That is foul, Pops. Klayton wasn't at the hospital because he loves her. He was up there because of his guilty conscience. He knew that it was his fault that she was laid up there and—" My father wouldn't even let me finish what I had to say, which was rude. I was trying to tell him about Klayton not being so innocent after all, but he wasn't listening to a word that I had to say.

"Luca Glover, I have had enough of your disrespectful shit. You need to get your shit in order before you sit there and judge others on your fucking high horse. Klayton had no idea that explosion was going to happen because he wouldn't have had Treasure in that house if he had known. If anyone is living with a guilty conscience, it is you, and there is no reason for you to live that way. Blach raping Treasure was never your fault, and I need you to get help to deal with your issues. If you don't, you might permanently damage your relationship with Treasure for good. You also have to let AJ go before you lose any chance at happiness that you have left. I am pissed that you ran Gigi out of here because she was good for you, and you should be focused on trying to fix things with her." My father looked sad.

The last thing that I wanted was for him to feel sorry for me. Honestly, my relationship with Treasure is already damaged and it broke my heart. I wanted to have that bond with her that I used to have.

"I know my house isn't in order, but Treasure was foul for even fucking with Klayton on some disloyal shit. She knew how I felt about him and—"

I was cut off by a slap in the face. I was startled to see Treasure had come out of her room.

Whap! Whap!

"Listen, Luca. I love you more than life itself, but you are not going to disrespect Klayton. Klayton and I might be broken up right now, but that man was there for me when I was in my coma and you weren't. Klayton and I will eventually work past the issues we got going on, but where in the fuck were you? Let me guess, you were busy drowning your sorrows in work because that is the only way you can cope with your feelings. I am tired of living in a bubble because that is what makes you feel comfortable. Life is too damn short for me to be miserable and I'm going to start living life for me whether you like it or not, Luca."

Treasure called herself bossing up on me, but it was time for me to tell her about herself. "Listen, little girl. You are one sorry, ungrateful bitch. Everything I have been doing is to make sure you and Genesis are good. I know that it appears foul that I didn't visit you a lot at the hospital, but I couldn't take seeing you in that condition. I know that it sounds selfish."

"It sounds selfish because it is, Luca! You are sitting here throwing stones at Klayton but no matter how hard it got for him, he showed up to visit me every day. Do you know how hard it was for him to see me in that damn condition?"

"Bitch, why are you defending a man that ain't shit? He was getting his mic blown by my ex-girlfriend in the fucking club and you still here defending his ass! Did you even see this picture?" I grabbed my phone and shoved it in her face. Treasure hasn't been here obviously, so she wouldn't know that the woman in the picture was my girlfriend. It looked like she was going to be sick but trying to maintain her composure. She was doing a lousy job of that.

"Luca, you claim you want me to be happy, but you want to shove bullshit in my face. I already know about the text message, which is why I broke up with him. I didn't bother to get a good look at the female in the picture, but she isn't my problem. Klayton owed me his loyalty, not her. The same way you owed me loyalty and didn't even show up more than once when I was in the hospital. In my eyes, you and Klayton are both fraud as hell. Your sins are different, but one isn't worse than the other. I can at least say Klayton fucked up, but what excuse can I say for you?" Treasure pointed her finger in my face. Our father quickly got in between us, things were getting heated.

"Are you really that pathetic, Treasure? Are you that desperate to have a man that you will settle for any ole game a nigga spit at you? Klayton isn't in love with you. He is attracted to you because you are the forbidden fruit and the woman that is off limits to him. What do you have that is any different from any other bitch out there? I hate to break it to you, Treasure, but you aren't special and those tears you were just crying over Klayton is proof of that." I stared at her.

"Luca, I fucking hate you and as soon as our parents' house is ready, I'm moving in with them!" Treasure cried and then ran out of the room.

I should have felt bad for how I talked to my sister, but I didn't. I wanted her to get it in her head that Klayton would never be able to love her the way that she deserved to be loved. It would hurt now, but she would thank me for giving her this cruel reality check in the long run.

"Luca, you really need to apologize for how you spoke to your sister. She really did not deserve that. We will all be out of your house soon because you have lost your fucking mind."

My father stared at me disappointed before he walked off. I was relieved because I needed some time to think about everything that went down but unfortunately, my mom came in soon after that. At first, she just stared at me before shaking her head at me.

"Luca, you are my first-born child, and I will always love you. I am disappointed in you for how you are acting. We are family and we are supposed to be better than this. I am sure that you do things that Treasure would not approve of, yet she doesn't judge you for it."

"I am her big brother, and she is supposed to listen to me. I know what is best for her and this is all coming from a place of love."

"Love doesn't hurt, Luca. You really don't think about what you say. If Klayton isn't the one for her then you need to let Treasure find that out on her own and not break her down over her own decisions. Getting hurt is a part of life and she needs your support, not your judgment. You can't protect her from everything in life. What you are doing is hurting her more. Think about what I said, son."

My mom walked off and left me to my thoughts. Was I really a terrible person for wanting to make sure that my sister was safe? All I knew was that nigga, Klayton Jackson, was not good for her and if I had to force her hand then I would. I prayed that it did not come down to forcing her to choose between me and Klayton because our brother-sister relationship just might not survive that blow.

4

BRII

I woke up to flashing lights and beeping. I was disoriented and had no idea where I was at.

"She's awake! All of the drugs are out of her system," a strange voice announced and then I remembered what happened.

I had tried to kill myself by taking a bunch of pills and mixing it with alcohol but obviously, my attempt failed. *I should have used a gun or a knife even though I was scared of pain,* I thought. I finally opened my eyes. I could tell that I was at a hospital and saw a bunch of medical personnel staring back at me. I hated hospitals, and I hated the fact that I was hospitalized. I should have made sure I finished the job when I had the chance. One of the nurses held a glass of water up to my pale lips and I gratefully took a sip of the water.

"I'm glad you are still with us ma'am. You have some people in the waiting room that are very concerned about you. You are lucky to have people that love and care about you in your corner. I don't know why you did what you did, but know that your life has a purpose, sweetie. I am nurse Stephanie Williams and if you need to talk later on, I am here for you." She walked out of the room and not long after that, a doctor walked into the room.

"Brinisha Lyons? You are one very lucky woman. The number of pills that you took should have been lethal enough to kill you. I am Doctor Martinez, and I will be your doctor for now until we complete your transfer to the psych ward for a psychiatric evaluation."

I tried to speak but started coughing. Even with the water I had consumed, my throat was still burning. "Excuse me? The psych ward?" It took everything in me to get those words out and another nurse came in and started giving me a little bit more water to drink.

"Mrs. Lyons, you tried to attempt suicide, and we cannot allow you to leave if you are a danger to yourself or others. This is for your own good ma'am." Doctor Martinez looked sympathetic. I wondered if the doctor was calling me a weak bitch in his head and only staying professional because his job called for professionalism.

I was pissed off because I didn't belong with any crazy people. I was perfectly sane and had a brief lapse of judgment. I felt bad for the kids and Jonah. Speaking of Jonah, something in my soul told me that something was terribly wrong. I prayed that Jonah didn't find me in that condition. We might have had our problems, but that wasn't something I would want for him to find.

"I don't want to go be with crazy people," I whispered. I know I had a lapse in judgment, but there was no reason to lock me up with other crazy people. I was perfectly fine, and I just wanted to be discharged so I could go back to living a normal life.

"I understand that you don't want to go to the psych ward, but you have no other choice. I am placing you on a 5250 hold which is good for the next seventy-two hours. During that time, there will be a psychiatric evaluation done and if everything checks out, they will discharge you. I don't know what led you to this point, but suicide is not the answer. There are a couple of people that are here to see you. I will let them come back here for a few minutes, but you need your rest. Once your visitors leave, we will have a psychiatrist come down to do the evaluation and then you can rest. Please press the red button if you need anything," Doctor Martinez gestured before leaving the room.

I was excited because I just knew that Jonah was here visiting me, and I was hopeful that we would be able to put all of the past drama behind us. I was slightly disappointed to see that it wasn't my husband walking in the room. I needed him right now more than anyone knows.

A couple of minutes later, Nikki and Kobe walked into the room. What scared me was they both looked like they had been crying, and Kobe wasn't the type of nigga to cry. Something told me that I was going to hear some very bad news soon. Nikki glared at me angrily, and I wasn't sure why I was the source of her anger, but I was sure that I was about to find out.

"Who took a shit in your cheerios?" I asked. Kobe shook his head and walked out of the room. I wasn't sure what the hell that was about. Maybe Nikki was tired of watching the kids for us and if so, I would try to find someone else to take them until I got out of here.

"I hope you realize that every action has a consequence, Brii. I should be happy that you are ok, but I wish you did die when you tried to kill yourself."

Nikki's hands were visibly shaking, and she couldn't maintain eye contact with me for very long. Nikki clearly has some beef with me, but I wasn't sure what it was. She was lucky my ass couldn't get out of this bed and beat her ass. I was not taking any disrespect from anyone.

"Would you please stop speaking in riddles, Nikki? Say what you got to say or get the fuck out!" I snapped. I had no reason to be angry at Nikki, but I was mad. I was mad that my suicide attempt failed, and I was still stuck on this planet. I already didn't want to be here, but I was also sick of her speaking in riddles. Get to the fucking point and get out so I can be alone.

"Bitch, it's your fault that Jonah died! He found your body lying in the damn bathroom and ended up shooting himself at point blank range in front of me and Kobe. You fucking killed Jonah!" Nikki screamed and I felt like this was all a nightmare. How the hell did my suicide attempt fail yet Jonah succeeded on his? God must have been playing a cruel trick on me because I didn't understand how things turned out this way.

"Please tell me you are joking, Nikki."

"I wouldn't joke about anything this serious, Brii. I know you and Jonah had marital problems, but that man loved you. He literally died for you, Brii, and now there is nothing that will bring him back. I hope you can live with yourself." Nikki's lips trembled and tears slid down her cheeks.

"My husband is dead. Nooooooo! What happened?" I screamed and realized that my body was restrained to my hospital bed like a chained up animal. Part of me wanted to know the details, but another part of me didn't because it would scar me for life.

"Fuck you, Brii. Do you know what it was like to watch Jonah put that gun to his fucking head? That is something that I will never forget for the rest of my life. That man grabbed a gun and shot himself in the head before Kobe or I could even stop him all because he thought you were dead. I fucking hate your selfish ass, Brii. Forget that we were ever sisters. Do you think that you were the first woman to ever get date raped? You are the weakest bitch that I know, but karma is a bitch. God knew what he was doing because you are going to have to live with the fact that you caused Jonah's death for the rest of your life. I never want to speak to you again unless it has something to do with the kids. I hope they lock you up in a mental hospital for the rest of your life!" Nikki spat. Nikki had every right to be in her feelings but hell, so did I. At the end of the day, I am Jonah's wife, and I would blame myself for the rest of my life.

Her words were like continuous punches to an already bruised body. How was I supposed to know that Jonah was going to react the way that he did? I opened my mouth to reply but no words would come out. I wanted to claim that it wasn't my fault, but I knew if I didn't try to do what I did then Jonah would still be alive.

"I-I'm sorry." My lips trembled, and I just stared at Nikki.

It was crazy because I didn't owe Nikki an apology, but I found myself giving her one anyways. All our lives had irrevocably changed and that was all attributed to my selfish actions. No matter how many ways you cut it, Jonah's blood was on my hands and karma truly was a bitch.

"Why are you here, Nikki?" I asked.

The wounds were way too fresh to sit here and listen to Nikki verbally abuse me. Deep down, a lot of that was hurt and grief, but it was more than I could bear at the moment. If she hates me the way that she says, I didn't understand why she was here. I didn't notice that Kobe had come back in the room until he started speaking.

"We both just wanted to make sure that you are ok. Nikki doesn't mean what she just said, and emotions are high right now."

"Emotions are high? I just found out my fucking husband died, and your wife is sitting here blaming me for the shit. How the hell can I be ok if she is here blaming me for his death? You guys see that I'm alive and well, now you can go. I have enough to deal with right now, and I don't need to hear any shit from you guys even if I do deserve it. No matter how I felt about Jonah lately, I never would have wanted him to kill himself over me."

"Bitch, it's your fault! You just don't want to take responsibility for your actions. You got the right one today. Did Jonah mess up and handle things wrong? Yes, he did, but you also lied to that man about being raped. His blood is on your hands, whore!" Nikki raged.

I didn't want to understand her anger, but I did because it is one thing to be in the streets catching bodies, but to watch someone shoot themselves in the head is horrifying. I knew she was grieving from what she had witnessed but damn, this was too much for me to deal with right now. I reached over to press the button for the nurse to come. I needed them to get security and get Nikki and Kobe out of my hospital room before the situation gets worse than it already was.

"Nikki, I didn't think how my actions would affect him and my kids and—"

"Excuse me, did you call for a nurse? I also heard some yelling coming from this room, so I was about to check on you anyways," Stephanie frowned at us.

"Yes, thank you for coming to check on me. Can you please get security to escort them out of here? I'm tired, and I need to rest," I told the nurse.

"You are a pussy ass bitch, Brii, to call security to escort us out. I don't want to be here anyways and I have been in much better company. Come on, Kobe, let's go. Just so you know, you better pray if you ever want to see Antoinette, Blake, or Leslie ever again."

5

GIOVANNI

I hated to get in Luca's ass the way that I did, but it was necessary. Hope had told me that Treasure wants to move in with us at our new house, and I was in full agreeance. Luca and Treasure couldn't be in the same room together. I wasn't happy learning that Klayton had cheated on my daughter. I was going to have some words for him the next time I talked to him. For now, it was time to do damage control and with Luca cutting up, I was thinking maybe we should go to a hotel for a night or two until the house was ready to move in. It hurt me to see my son hurting the way that he has been. I just wanted both of my kids and my granddaughter to be happy.

I went into Genesis' room. Seeing Hope playing with Genesis, a smile played on my lips. I wanted us all to go back to being a happy family, but I had a feeling that we were right in the middle of a storm. "Hope, can I talk to you for a moment?" I asked. I said hello to Genesis and she said hello back to me.

"Sure, let me see if Treasure is up to playing with Genesis real quick." Hope got up and went to go get our daughter. That was another issue that we needed to work through as a family. I know that Treasure originally wanted to get an abortion when she was pregnant with Genesis. However, Genesis is here now, and I was starting to feel like she deserved to know that Treasure is her mother even if Hope and I continued raising her. That was a conversation I wanted to have with Treasure on a later date.

Treasure walked in the room, and I felt bad because I knew that she had been crying. This was one of the times I was relieved that Genesis couldn't see because she didn't need to know that she had been crying.

"I can stay with her for the rest of the day. You and mom have been amazing, and I love you guys. I need to do better with spending more time with Genesis," Treasure replied quietly. My daughter has been through more than any ordinary twenty-one year old should have to go through. I would do anything to see my daughter live a long and happy life.

"I love you, baby doll, and we will get through this as a family. If you have a chance to, start packing some toys and extra clothes for Genesis in a bag. I think we will go to a hotel until the new house is ready. I can't have you two staying here while Luca is around here acting crazy."

I hugged Treasure and walked out of the room. I went into the guest room where I saw Hope waiting for me. I was grateful to get a second chance at love with Hope even though we had a long rocky road to get here.

"What's going on, Gio?" Hope looked up at me, and I could tell she was tired. Truth be told, I was tired of all of this drama too, but someone had to stay strong right now.

"Go pack Treasure's bag. I booked a room at the Four Seasons until our house is ready. This isn't going to work, and Treasure and Luca need some space from each other." I walked over and held my wife in my arms. I never take Hope for granted because my father kept us apart for years and the damage from that still had an impact on the Glover family.

"Ok, babe. I'm worried about Luca. He really needs help before he ends up self-destructing," Hope admitted, and she started crying.

I wasn't sure how much more this family could take, and I prayed Luca got help and became the man that I know that he can be. I felt helpless as a man because I didn't protect my family years ago and they were still hurting now. How could I convince Luca's prideful ass to get the help that he needed?

Some of you might be wondering what happened to Jeremiah from Coke Gurls Cali. He ended up wanting to go live with a family on his mother's side of the family. I haven't talked to him in the last two years, but I always made it known that I would be there for him. Part of me thinks that he blames me for his mother, Victoria's, death even though she dug her own grave.

"I know, babe, but we can't force Luca to get help. I have been researching different counselors and they have said they can do a consultation with us for family counseling, but we can't force him into any individual counseling with him being an adult. We have to continue praying that he comes to his senses soon and wakes up. It feels horrible to know that Luca has his issues because of decisions that I made when we were younger."

"Gio, you did the best you could, honey. You wanted to keep us safe and I love you for that, so don't blame yourself—"

Hope was interrupted by the phone ringing. I saw Kobe Jackson's number on my phone and held my hand up to quiet Hope. If one of the Jackson brothers were calling, it was for a good reason.

"Hello?" I answered. I could hear his wife crying in the background, and I knew that something was terribly wrong. The last thing that we needed was more bad news.

"Giovanni, Jonah is dead," Those were the first words out of Kobe's mouth, and I was shocked.

"Say that again? You gotta be joking. What the hell happened to Jonah?" I asked. Luca was already not in a good head space, but when he finds out that Jonah passed away, he was really going to lose it.

"Jonah shot himself in the head and killed himself. He did it right in front of Nikki and I. We just left the hospital from visiting Brii," Kobe admitted. I had so many questions and my head was spinning. What in the sam hell was going on?

"That doesn't even sound like Jonah. Listen, let me get Hope and the girls settled at a hotel and then I will meet you at your house. I have questions and this is a conversation that needs to be done in person," I insisted and hung up on Kobe.

When it rains, it fucking pours. It was taking everything in me to stay strong right now. Hope was staring at me. I knew that she wanted to know what the fuck was going on. There was no time for that now. I would get her up to speed once I knew what was going on.

"Hope, get Treasure and Genesis. We got to go now," I ordered.

I grabbed the keys to the rental car and Hope followed behind me. I went to go start the car and a few minutes later, the girls came out. Treasure made sure Genesis was strapped in the car securely. I didn't bother to say anything to Luca yet because he wasn't in a good head space and when I did break the news to him, I wanted to have all of the facts straight. I was dreading having to tell Luca because he was one screw away from becoming completely unhinged.

I drove off quickly and went to check the girls into the hotel. Two hours later, I was finally pulling up to Kobe Jackson's house, and I dreaded going inside. Something told me that I wasn't ready for what I was about to find out. I reluctantly got out the car and went to ring the doorbell, but Kobe answered the door before I could ring it. There were toys and different things on the floor but considering the circumstances, I understood the house being messy.

"Thanks for coming, Giovanni. Trayce and Rolonda have all of the kids, so it's just me, you and Nikki here. Let me go get us some Henny because we are going to need it. Please make yourself comfortable in the living room," Kobe told me, and I went to do just that.

Kobe came in with two shot glasses, and I could hear Nikki screaming and crying from upstairs. "What happened?" I asked in a no-nonsense manner.

"Man, shit has been hitting the fan. Bare with me because this all explains what lead up to Jonah's death," Kobe explained, and I nodded my head in agreement.

"Keep going," I coached him. It was tough losing someone else who was like family and it took me back to AJ's death.

"Brii was date raped and lied to Jonah about it. She claimed that she cheated on him when he dragged her out of an abortion clinic.

He didn't find out she lied about cheating until he went home to get some things and overheard Brii and Ro arguing about telling Jonah the truth."

"Man, this sounds like some fucking Maury type of shit."

"I'm getting there, Giovanni. Anyways, Jonah was thrown off and apparently, he was distant from Brii after that. She was having a hard time coping, and we all drove to their house to check on Brii. Nikki and I had been watching the kids for them since they had been having marital problems. Jonah found her body in the bathroom because Brii overdosed on pills. He thought Brii was dead and ended up shooting himself in the head right in front of me and my wife. Nikki and I just came from visiting Brii in the hospital, and they have her on a psychiatric hold since she tried to kill herself. Nikki blamed Brii for Jonah's death but honestly, Brii has been in a bad spot for a while now. Shit hit the fan at the hospital, and I had to drag Nikki out of there," Kobe explained, and my mouth dropped open. I couldn't believe all of this was going on.

"What in the hell am I going to tell Luca? There is no way that he is going to take Jonah's death well at all. He is barely hanging on to sanity as it is since AJ died three years ago, so I know that he isn't going to take this well. Thank you for keeping the kids. I know this hasn't been easy on you and Nikki." I gave Kobe a hug.

"Man, we are all going to need to keep an eye on Luca and try to encourage him to get the help that he needs. He is going to need all of the support to get through this."

6

KLAYTON

"Klayton Jackson? My name is Sparkle Lewis, and I'm your CPS worker. I'm here on behalf of Danielle Jackson. I would like to speak with you for a minute?" Sparkle asked politely.

What kind of fucking name is Sparkle? It sounds like a stripper name, and I bet she has been on some damn stripper pole before working for child services. She was dressed professionally and had her long red hair tied up in a ponytail. She is a beautiful woman, but a nigga like me sees bad bitches every day of the week, so I wasn't moved by Sparkle's beauty. I really didn't want to talk to the bitch, but I knew I had no other choice. Losing my daughter to the system was simply not an option. Skittles, Sparkle, or whatever her name was, is gonna learn that I am not the nigga she wants to play with.

"Klayton, you guys should go to the cafeteria and have a coffee. If there is any news on Danielle, I promise I will call you," Ro reassured me. Ro could tell I was reluctant to go with her, and Trayce walked over and gave me a brotherly hug.

"Don't let that hoe see you sweat. Everything is going to be just fine. Remember the custody of your daughter is at stake, so stay calm, nigga. Shoot me a 911 text if you need me because I know how you get," Trayce whispered and he let me go.

"Fine. Let's make this quick. I know you have a job to do, and I will explain everything that happened. But after that, I need to be up here waiting for news on my daughter." I reluctantly gave in and lead Sparkle to the cafeteria. We got in line and grabbed some coffee and snacks, or I should say she grabbed some snacks. I paid for the items, and we sat down at a table in the corner where we could talk privately.

"Klayton, I can tell that you love your daughter very much, and I know this is a very difficult time for you—"

"Cut the small talk and get down to business. Better yet, let me tell you what happened so I can save us both some fucking time. My girlfriend and I were arguing, and she got emotional. She grabbed a gun and threatened to shoot me. I was trying to talk her down and neither of us realized that my daughter woke up from her nap and walked into the room. The gun went off, and I thought Danielle got shot. When I went to grab her, it turned out she fell and hit her head due to the sound of the gun and wasn't shot. It was an accident, and I am an excellent father—"

"Listen, I am sure you are an excellent father. You appear to love your daughter a lot and I feel for you. However, this was an act of negligence and the gun never should have been out, especially knowing you have a four-year-old child in the home that could wake up at any time. The other issue I have is technically your girlfriend would have committed domestic violence, and I can have Danielle removed from your care off of that alone. I have been a CPS worker for three years now, Klayton, and I have seen a lot working in this field. My job is to do what is best for Danielle."

"What the fuck does that have to do with anything? I don't give a fuck how long you been doing your job, but what you are not going to do is take my child away from me even if I have to body your ass and your entire family to do it! I do not play about mine, and I am offended at the fact that you are insinuating that my child is being neglected." I was tempted to choke this hoe, but I could hear Trayce in my head telling me to stay cool, calm and collected. I was tempted to go back to being reckless Klayton and if Danielle was taken from me, I was going to make the entire state of California feel me.

"Listen, nigga, you don't have to get rude or disrespectful. Don't let this outfit fool you because I can get ghetto and disrespectful with you." Sparkle snapped her fingers in my face, and I was on the verge of losing it.

"Listen, you Ronald Mcdonald looking clown. What you are not going to do is disrespect me and make me feel like I am not a good father. I would give my fucking life for Danielle, and I already kicked my girlfriend out of my house for what happened. What you are not going to do is guilt trip me and hold shit over my fucking head. My child will always come first, point, blank, period." I checked her ass real quick. I threw my empty coffee cup and started to walk back to Danielle's hospital room. As far as I was concerned, this conversation was over.

"I highly suggest you get your ass back here because I hold the fate of your daughter in my hands. I have the power to put her in the system, let her stay with relatives of yours, or let you keep her. You need to lower your attitude because I am just doing my job. It is my job to get the facts of what happened, conduct an investigation, and make a decision on what is best for the child. Now you can get out of your feelings and work with me on this investigation, or I can make a decision based off of what I do know. And you won't like the decision that I make," Sparkle warned me. If the situation wasn't as severe as it was, I would have shoved my dick down her throat and fucked her face.

I hated the fact that she has control in this situation because I am not the type of nigga to back down for no one. However, I would do anything for my daughter. So, if I had to feed this woman's ego for a bit, then so be it.

"I gave you the facts of what happened. What I am not going to do is sit here and argue fucking semantics with you when it appears that you already have your mind made up anyways." I sat back down in my seat.

"Listen, Klayton. I understand this is a difficult time for you and it would be for any parent that loves their kid. The one thing that I don't question is your love for Danielle, but you also have to let me do my job. It is refreshing to see a father who actually cares about his child because I see so many deadbeat parents that leave their children in bad situations, so I know this is difficult for you. I actually care about my job and the children that are voiceless so I try to speak on their behalf. With that being said, I do not want to take Danielle from you, but I also cannot live with giving her back to your care right away. I have seen so many parents choose their spouse over their kids and—"

"I get where you are coming from and I admire your passion for your job. However, my name is Klayton mothafucking Jackson, and you will put some respect on my name. I am not every other nigga out there that would put a bitch before their kid. Like I told you before, shit is done with me and Treasure, and my priority is Danielle. Don't judge me by every other case that you have dealt with because that is not fair to me or my daughter," I stated confidently. Ironically, this was a time that I felt anything but confident. I could end up losing my child and that had me scared more than anything I ever dealt with in the streets.

"Listen, this is off the record, but it is obvious your ass is in the streets. Have you ever thought about leaving that life alone? If your daughter is truly your priority then you will make changes to your lifestyle," Sparkle called herself lecturing me, but how I make my money is none of her business. My lifestyle wasn't what got my daughter caught up although technically it could be blamed albeit indirectly.

"No disrespect, but my lifestyle isn't the reason my daughter is in the hospital. We are here to discuss the CPS case that you have opened against me, nothing more and nothing less. You need to decide what you are going to do, and we can move forward. Yes, my fate is in your hands, but I am not going to keep kissing your ass when you are likely going to put my daughter in the system anyways. Every other nigga might be kissing your ass in this situation, but I am not going to and that is what has you upset. Now I saw you clocking a nigga's dick, and I can bless you with some dick if that is what your thirsty ass is after."

"Me thirsty? Never that, nigga. Just know that if you were ever blessed to get in between my legs, that will be because your ass is pressed for pussy. You are not the only fine ass nigga out here, Klayton."

"I might not be the only one, but I know that super soaker you got is wet as fuck right now. You look out for me and I look out for you," I suggested. I knew dick was her end game. When you got good dick and is fine as fuck like my ass is, hoes will use any way to worm their way in their life. Sparkle might not be a yes woman right off the top, but I knew the type of time she was on. Game recognizes game.

"Look, the most I can do for you is do a home inspection of your brother's house. If everything checks out, and that is a big IF, then I will release temporary custody to your brother." Sparkle stared at me and her face was still flushed from the way I had been talking to her. We both knew what it was. If I even put in the slightest bit of effort, I could have her outside busting it open for a real nigga.

I wasn't thrilled about what she was saying but after thinking about it, what Sparkle was saying made sense. The best place for Danielle would be with my brother until I caught up to Kamar and made that nigga pay with his life. I knew that my daughter would be safe with my brother and that was better than letting her go in the system. I needed to know what I needed to do to make sure I could get permanent custody of Danielle back. I might not be retiring from the streets anytime soon, but Danielle was going to be made a priority once I finally got rid of Kamar.

"I appreciate that. I do not want my daughter going into the system. For one, she is accustomed to the lifestyle that I provide for her. Secondly, I don't want her living with any random strangers that could abuse or hurt her. Surely you can understand that. A lot of these foster parents only take in children for the paycheck that they get from it and don't care about the child's welfare. I would hate to have to catch unnecessary bodies behind my daughter, but I will if I have to." I made sure she understood the hidden threat in my message. The only difference was, I don't normally make threats. I make promises.

"I get that you want her to be safe and that is the end goal for me too. Danielle's safety and well-being is my main priority. As I said, this will only be temporary and once I feel like it is safe to give your permanent custody of your daughter back, I will. This is the best case scenario for all parties involved because you obviously love your daughter. You place a lot of confidence in your brother and of course, I want to talk to him, but I do not like having to remove children unless it is necessary. In this case, you have a good enough support system that I can trust with Danielle's care so I don't have to remove her. You wouldn't believe it, but I do not like having to uproot children from their homes and that is why I am giving this a lot of consideration. Hell, I normally wouldn't even give someone more than once to disrespect me before I make my decision, but I also understand that you are reacting out of fear of losing your child. Do not make me regret my decision. Now let's go talk to your brother and find out what is going on with Danielle's condition."

7

TREASURE

I was relieved to get out of Luca's house even though I had only gone back temporarily. I love my older brother but I needed him to get help to deal with the demons that he was fighting so we could be a family again. I wasn't sure how much more I could take from his ass, and I needed to bond more with my daughter anyways. I was taking this time away from Klayton to figure myself out and be selfish for a bit. It was time for me to put my daughter and myself first while I prove to everyone that I could be the mother to Genesis that she deserved. Genesis and I were sharing a suite and my parents shared the other one. I knocked on the door to check on my mom since Genesis had fallen asleep. I had spent the last ten minutes watching her sleep.

My daughter is such a blessing. When I look at Genesis, I see a lot of my own features. I was relieved to see that my love for Genesis outweighs any of my past feelings that I had whenever I looked at her. I didn't see Blach anymore when I look at her, but I was happy that Genesis took on more of my features than his. Hopefully, my daughter would never have any of his evil ways.

My mom opened the connecting door between our rooms and walked into mine. "Hey, baby. Is Genesis sleep yet?"

"Yes, she is tired, mom. Come have a drink with me."

I walked over to the mini bar and grabbed a small bottle of vodka. I wasn't going to drink too much since my daughter was with me, but I needed a shot to take the edge off of things. I probably shouldn't have been drinking, but I wasn't taking my medication for my schizophrenia, so having one drink wouldn't kill me. Right now, there was a lot on my mind, especially the fact that Klayton cheated on me.

"You go ahead and have a drink, baby doll. Now how are you feeling about everything?" My mom asked me. I stared at her and it looked like she had been crying again. Something was going on with my mother and I wanted to find out what it was. I felt bad because I know she worries about me a lot and I needed to take some stress off of her plate.

"I'm fine. Mom, what is going on with you? You think I didn't notice, but I know you have been crying. I'm worried about you," I admitted.

"Baby, there is a storm coming for this family and I am not sure if we are going to make it through."

My mom was breaking my heart and I knew that something serious was bothering her. When would all of the drama end? I just wanted my family to be happy and enjoy life together.

"Mom, I love you and I'm here for you. You can tell me what's going on." I wanted my mother to be able to confide in me. Whatever was going on with her, we would get through it together.

"I know you and Luca aren't getting along right now, but we are going to have to put that aside for now. Luca is going to need us to be there for him no matter how much he pushes us away. Your dad found out some terrible news earlier." My mom started crying. I was getting a little impatient and wanted to know what it was, but I also knew that my mother would reveal it on her time.

"Mom, what is going on?" I had a sick feeling that things were about to take a turn for the worst and when I heard the next words come out of my mom's mouth, I knew I was right.

"Jonah died, sweetie, and Luca doesn't know. Your father went to go talk to Kobe who was the one that called and gave him the news."

My mouth dropped because I didn't see that coming. "Omg! Luca is going to fucking lose it. Maybe I should go back home because he is going to need us and—"

"Treasure, no. You don't need to be in his warpath when he finds this news out. You need to be with Genesis. She needs to be your primary concern right now, even above your brother. We are going to be here for Luca and I don't know how we are going to tell him."

My mom broke down, and I wrapped my arms around her. I forced myself to push Klayton out of my mind because right now, my family needed me. I had to put my big girl panties and find a way to be there for Luca and my parents. I knew watching Luca's mental health deteriorate was already taking a toll on them.

"Do you know any details? Jonah is like his brother. Luca is going to really lose his mind after this," I whispered more so to myself and I started crying for him. No matter what Luca and I go through, at the end of the day, we ride hard for each other. Our family might be dysfunctional as hell, but I prayed Jonah's death would help bring us together. However, I was scared that it would push us further apart. Luca was already self-destructing, but this news would fucking break my brother.

"No, he went to Kobe's house and has been gone for a while—" My mom was interrupted by my father walking in my room. He gathered us in his arms, and we all cried together. Jonah was like a brother to me, but there was no time for me to grieve over his loss. I was going to have to be strong for Luca right now.

"Dad, who is going to tell Luca? I will tell him if you guys need me to. I just don't think he will listen to anything I have to say. You guys have been here for me through everything the last few years, so if you want me to go and tell him, I will. Maybe this will be what Luca needs to get help." I was trying to stay strong, but it was hard. This was the elephant that needed to be addressed in the room. Hell, I would do it, but I doubt Luca would listen to anything I had to say since we had our argument.

"I love you girls so much. I appreciate you volunteering and being selfless, Treasure. I know that isn't easy for you. I think what would be better is if you stay here and bond with Genesis. You might trigger Luca and your daughter needs to be your first priority. Your mom and I can go deal with Luca together and hopefully, we can encourage him to go get help. By the way, I owe you an apology, Treasure," my dad began. I was confused. Why would my father apologize to me? He did nothing wrong.

"Dad, did you smoke some weed at Kobe's house? You don't owe me an apology. Stop smoking the good shit," I dismissed his apology.

"Hear me out, Treasure. Hope and I both did you a disservice when everything went down with Blach. I love my granddaughter and I don't regret her one bit, honey. However, I do regret the fact that we disregarded your feelings about the pregnancy. It was your body and it should have been your decision to make. Now you are struggling with guilt because you aren't as involved with your daughter like other mothers. I don't want you to feel that guilt anymore, Treasure. Hope and I knew what we were getting ourselves into when we forced you to have her, and we also knew there was a possibility that you would never be able to raise Genesis because she would be a constant reminder of your trauma."

"Dad, I love you and mom to pieces. I don't regret how things happened because everything happens for a reason. Genesis was meant to be here and if I did go through with the abortion, that is something I would have had to live with for the rest of my life. I want to and I need to prove to you guys, and to myself, that I am capable of raising Genesis. Luca is right about one thing. I need to woman up and take care of my own responsibilities. I need to focus on putting Genesis first and allow you guys to live your best lives. You shouldn't have to raise my child for me. I know you guys don't mind, but I do want to get full custody of her soon. I don't care if I have to get a job and go to school. I want to be independent and be a better mother," I admitted.

"We are here for you every step of the way. Don't do anything because you feel like you have to do it. We are in no rush and we knew what we were getting into. Now, does Klayton have anything to do with this desire to raise Genesis?" My mom asked me.

I sat and thought carefully before I answered. "He does, but he inspires me to be a better mother and get my shit together. Genesis deserves it and she deserves to know who her mother is. The truly innocent one in all of this is Genesis and that is whose feelings should be considered the most. I need to do better, and I am going to be a permanent presence in her life. One day you guys will be gone, and she needs to know that I will be there for her. Now I will say this in regards to my brother. I love him, but I don't think he should be around Genesis right now until he is emotionally stable. The last thing I need is for Luca to scare Genesis," I insisted and now I could understand more why Klayton reacted the way he did over what happened to Danielle.

"That is why you should stay with Genesis and start to spend more time with her and build that relationship with her. Hope and I can deal with handling Luca. Just know that we love you guys so much, and it hurts us to see you guys hurting. The same way that we love you and Luca, we love Genesis. She needs stability, Treasure, and you really need to sit back and think whether you will get in a position where you will take full care of her. It is unfair to her with all of the back and forth and like you said, she is the one who is truly innocent in all of this. Genesis needs and deserves stability. Right now, you are trying to figure out your relationship with Klayton and finish school. I don't want you to take on too much. Your dad and I will understand and love you regardless of what you decide," my mom encouraged me.

Deep down, I knew she was right, and it wasn't fair for me to go in and out of Genesis' life. This paved the way for the next part of our conversation, and I wasn't sure how this was gonna go. "Speaking of Genesis, when do you think it is time to tell her that I am her mom? I know that I don't have full custody of her yet, but eventually, she needs to know. I would rather Genesis find this out when she is younger than when she gets older." I wanted to get my point across. I knew that I had no room to make demands, especially since I have a good support system with my parents. But the same way my parents had an opinion on my relationship with my daughter, I would give mine as well.

"Baby doll, she does deserve to know but right now, the main focus needs to be her stability. It might raise more questions and confusion if we tell Genesis now, especially since you have more of a distant relationship with her as it is. Genesis knows you as her sister, and we already have enough drama going on. I just don't think it is a good idea to tell her right now," my father let me down gently.

"I am not saying Genesis needs to know right this second. I just want us to work towards telling her the truth. My biggest fear is she gets older, finds out the wrong way and then ends up rebelling. I don't want her to cut up when she gets to be a teenager. She doesn't need to know the full story right now because Genesis is too young, but I don't think she should stay completely in the dark either," I explained.

"This is a conversation that we will all have to sit down with Genesis and have one day. Right now, we have enough drama on our plate to deal with. We have to decide once and for all on whether to let Genesis get the cornea transplant surgery." My mom looked at me.

"You are right. Speaking of that, I would like to go and meet her eye doctor when things settle down. If there is an opportunity that can potentially give my baby girl her vision back, I am all for looking into it."

8

GIGI

I miss Luca so much. I wish I could kick myself in the fucking foot for falling in love with my employer. I should have known better than to mix business with pleasure. A hard head makes a soft behind and this heartbreak was teaching me a valuable lesson. I had a feeling that Luca wasn't over AJ, and I value myself enough to not settle for second place. Besides, I had goals to achieve and love and marriage doesn't exactly fit into that picture right now. I wanted to get my career established and travel around the world. I wanted to live my best life drama free and it would be hard to do that if I let myself fall in love.

"Gigi, I'm here!" Candice announced. She walked into my hotel room bearing gifts. How the hell did my sister get a key to my hotel room? She must have bribed the person at the front desk. I was going to cuss them out later on.

"Go away, bih. I wanted to stay to myself and work on some client cases. Hell, I just woke up a few minutes ago," I complained. I love my sister, but I also like having my space. I am introverted by nature and happy with my own company.

"Naw, it's time to get your ass up. It's a nice sunny day in LA. We are going to go outside and lounge by the fucking pool. You can work on those damn cases later. I went and got a bathing suit for you and your favorite Chunky Monkey Ben and Jerry's ice cream, sis. You aren't getting rid of me, so you might as well go change. I got all day." Candice sat her happy ass on my bed. I got back on the other side of my bed and threw the covers on me. I didn't feel like being bothered, and she knows that I don't do anything that I don't want to do.

I was starting to fall back asleep when I felt cold water splash on my face. "Yo' what the fuck, Candice? I'ma beat your ass and you better not have gotten water on my fucking laptop!"

"Gigi, chill. I moved your laptop to the table over there. I meant what I said, and you know how annoying I can get until I get my way, so you might as well go and get ready."

I sat up and called the housekeeper to change the sheets and shit. I went and got dressed in the bathing suit Candice got me and put some shorts on my butt so I could be comfortable.

"I'm not going outside for long. I have cases to work on," I warned Candice. I guess you could say I'm a workaholic, and I truly enjoy what I do. That was the main reason I wasn't saying fuck Luca's law firm because no matter what, I wouldn't do his ass foul like that.

"Chill, sis. I just want to get you out of this stuffy ass room and spend some time with you. I won't even force you to talk about Luca because I have a feeling that nigga is why your ass is down in the fucking dumps."

"Don't mention his name," I warned my sister. It was bad enough that I still technically work for him. I didn't want to put more energy into him than necessary. In my eyes, our breakup was Luca's fault and if I confided in Candice, she would likely say some shit that I didn't want to hear.

Candice gave me a knowing look. "I'm here for you when you are ready to talk. Maybe some new dick will get you right."

"Hell naw. I'm good. Luca just can't get over his fucking past. Do I look like boo boo the fool? He is still mourning a damn ghost, and he even called me her name. It wasn't a good look for me to get involved with him in the first place, and I don't like light skinned niggas anyway. Luca has more skeletons than a little bit, and I'm not prepared to deal with all of his issues. He is a nice man, but he isn't for me," I admitted. I hated the fact that I felt things for him that I never felt with any other man, and I miss him more than I thought I would.

"Rewind, sis. Sit down while I make us some coffee. Now, what happened?" Candice asked in a no-nonsense manner. Hell, I thought she wanted to go out and now she doesn't want to leave?

"We got into a fight and Luca confided in me about his past. He told me how he lost the woman he was in love with in the past. I felt bad for him, but I also explained that I felt like he still wasn't over AJ and got defensive. I told him that we need some space, he got upset, and I ended up leaving his house. Now I'm hiding out from his ass. This emotional love shit isn't for me, sis. I just don't do feelings, and Luca makes me feel things that I shouldn't be feeling," I explained.

Candice set a piping hot cup of coffee in front of me with two creams and two sugars just the way that I liked it. Candice stared at me before shaking her head in obvious disapproval. "So, you mean to tell me that you get this nigga to open up about something that is personal to him and you punish him by breaking up with him? You are a special kind of stupid, sis."

"Who are you to judge me, sis? If you had heard the conversation, you would have understood why I felt insecure. And then he called me her name, AJ—"

"The real issue is you're running from love, Gigi. You're scared based off of your past with James that Luca is going to break your heart. You didn't even give the man a chance before you gave him an excuse so you could go running. You're in love with Luca and afraid to admit it. Of course, he still has love for his ex that died. They had a special connection, and he will always grieve her death. That doesn't mean he is still in love with AJ anymore though." Candice took a sip of her coffee. The way that Luca described AJ when he told me about her told me that he still has some kind of love for her. I just didn't want to compete with a ghost.

"I got to disagree. I do not want to be with a man where I feel like I have to compete for his affection. He is always going to be living through AJ's ghost and I refuse to try to live up to her. No disrespect to the dead but I don't need to be jealous of no damn ghost" I fussed.

"That is your insecurities talking. Do you really think Luca would have had you in his home with his family if he wasn't falling for you? He doesn't strike me as the kind of man that would have anyone around his family. You need to deal with your own issues and ask yourself why you are running from love. Stop punishing Luca for the past and allow him to love you." Candice hugged me.

Love doesn't pay the bills and love will have a person out there looking stupid like Marina. I love my best friend, but I don't want to be like her, accepting any kind of behavior just so I can say that I have a man.

"Sis, the only family I need is you real talk. I also get the sense that he has more issues than a little bit, and I don't know if I can deal with them," I admitted. I got up and threw my empty paper cup in the trash can. It was unfair for me to judge Luca considering I have a past myself, but there was something about loving Luca that scares me, and it just wasn't worth the risk.

"Who are you to judge? You have more issues than a little bit yourself? You have a hard time opening up and trusting others. You tend to run when things get tough, and your attitude isn't always easy to deal with. I think you and Luca can help each other heal. You two are good for each other, but only if you allow him to be there for you. Stop running and embrace the man that God made just for you," Candice announced.

"What about you, sis? When are you gonna settle down and get married?" I changed the subject because I was tired of being in the hot seat.

"Not anytime soon. You think your ass is slick, sis. You deserve to be happy, Gigi and I don't want you to waste your chance at happiness because you're too busy playing games and running from love. Not all men will do you the way James did," Candice schooled me.

"I know, but I need to keep my eye on the prize. My career won't break my heart, and I don't want us to ever struggle financially again. We have come a long way and men just aren't my focus right now.

Hell, look at how Anthony did Marina's ass. Sure, there are good men out there, but they are rare and hard to find."

"When you find you a good ass nigga, you hold on to him and not run from love, sis. Anthony and James are both co-captains in the fuck boy club, and we both know this. Yes, Luca could break your heart, but he could also be the one for you. Hell, the fact that the man is opening his heart to you means that he clearly cares about you, and I think you are dead ass wrong for how you handled the situation. I love you and I want you to be happy," Candice insisted. She was making some good points and giving me a lot to think about.

"Enough of that rah rah shit, sis. Let's go to the pool like you came over here to do. If Luca and I are meant to be, then we will work things out. If not, we just weren't meant to be, and I'm ok with that."

9

LUCA

My stubborn ass was missing Gigi, but a nigga was too stubborn to call her. Not to mention, Jonah hasn't been answering his phone, which was unlike him. I decided I was going to see if he went home to his old house. I got myself dressed and put my laptop away. My house was lonely now that my parents, niece, and sister were gone, and I missed them. Part of me was relieved because I needed the space so I could figure everything out. I heard the door open and I knew it had to have been my family. They left yesterday. I was surprised they popped up on me as quickly as they did.

"Luca, where are you at?" My father's voice echoed.

"I'm in my study, pops. Is everything ok?" I asked. I was angry at my sister, but I never wanted anything to happen to any of them.

My parents both walked into the room, and they looked stressed. My mom had been crying and I could tell because she had her usual sunglasses on when she had been going through it. My father looked like he was going through it too, and he had wrinkle lines that were visible on his face. Something told me that there was something terribly wrong, and I wasn't sure if I really wanted to know the bad news.

"Luca, come sit with me and your mom. We need to talk to you about something and it can't wait," my father replied.

I looked at him and was curious. What the hell was so important that it couldn't wait? I sat next to my parents and stared at them intently.

"Spit it out. What's up?"

My mom grabbed my hand and squeezed it. "Luca, you know that we love you and we are here for you? We will get through this as a family."

"Get through what? What the hell are you talking about?" I asked, confused. I had a feeling that I was not prepared for what I was about to find out. There has been too much going on lately, and I was afraid I wouldn't survive finding out any more bad news.

"Luca, be respectful to your mother!" My father yelled at me. I didn't mean to come out of pocket towards my mom, but I wanted to know what was up.

"Sorry, mom. What is the bad news?" I asked, suddenly more contrite.

"Baby, it's Jonah. He died—"

My mom didn't even finish what she was saying before I went the hell off. "No, he didn't die! This isn't a funny joke, Mom!" I yelled and stood up.

I stared at both of my parents' faces and neither of them looked like they were joking. In fact, my mom started crying again and it really started to hit me that my best friend, hell, my brother was really dead. It felt like the room was spinning, and I got dizzy. I couldn't have heard what my mom had just said. There has to be a mistake. This could not be true.

"Nooooooo!" I fell to my knees and was instantly devastated. It felt like all of the air was knocked out of me. How the hell did this happen? My entire world was crashing, and I felt like I was helpless to stop it. If anything, I should have died before Jonah did. Now that my brother was gone, I felt lost and alone. I still had my family, but there were just certain things I couldn't confide in them about. Jonah was simply irreplaceable.

I felt my parents wrap their arms around me, and I just laid there crying. I lost track of time. I couldn't believe Jonah was dead. I didn't even have the energy to ask how he died yet. I needed to know, yet I didn't want to know if that makes sense. "That is my brother. We were supposed to torment each other in the old folks home one day, man. I'm supposed to be able to talk shit about his weak ass jump shot and tell him the Lakers are better than the fucking Warriors, not hear that he is dead. This has to be a fucking nightmare. I need to wake up out of this."

My mom was rubbing my back and my father was doing his best to be there for me. "God called Jonah home, and I can't explain why. We will get through this together. I won't leave you son." I knew that my mother meant well, but there was no way that we would just simply get through this. Losing Jonah was even worse than losing AJ because of the history Jonah and I had together. He understood me in ways no one else did.

"Naw, man! Everyone I love fucking leaves me! Gigi left me, AJ left me, you left me when I was a baby, and now Jonah is gone! What did I do to deserve this kind of pain?" I sobbed and my heart was broken into a million different pieces. No one could convince me that Jonah's death wasn't my fault. I must have been some kind of a personal jinx to end up losing everyone that I cared about.

"Luca, we are here for you. I promise you your family is here, and we aren't going anywhere," my mom tried reassuring me, but nothing was working.

"Who the hell offed that nigga? That nigga just signed his death certificate and my ass is about to go back to being savage ass Hood and paint these streets red. These niggas must want this fucking smoke!" Jonah and I had a bond so deep that we would murk behind each other with no questions asked. Whoever the fuck did this was going to pay with their life.

"Listen, Jonah—"

"No, you listen, Pops! I tried doing things the right way. I went to law school, passed the bar and opened my law firm. I left the streets alone so mom wouldn't have to stress out about me dying in these streets, and death and bullshit still manage to follow me. Fuck doing things the right way. I'm about to give up my firm and get back to getting my hands dirty—"

"Luca, you know Jonah wouldn't want that for you. Calm down so we can talk about this, please. It hurts me to see you upset!" My mom begged. Normally, my mom's tears would be enough to make me think twice about cutting up, but right now I wasn't thinking straight. I couldn't handle losing another person that I cared about, and I barely recovered from losing AJ.

Losing Jonah reminded me of the dark days when I lost AJ and I would barely eat or drink anything. Jonah used to come and sit with me while I grieved over AJ. He wouldn't say much but just sit with me and be there for me like he has always been. Man, there were so many memories I have with my brother, and they were starting to play out like a movie in my head. I was having trouble dealing with the fact that my brother was really gone.

My parents continued holding me, but it didn't ease my pain. "How did he die? Don't hold anything back from me. I need to know how he died." I was trying to be calm, but the savage in me was waking up.

"Luca, don't do this to yourself, baby. You really don't want to know."

"Just tell me how my nigga died! I need to know. I'm going to find out one way or the other."

"Listen son. You are already hurting, and we don't want to overload you with too much at once," my father replied. I understood he was trying to protect me, but at this point, things couldn't get worse than they already were.

"How would you feel if someone close to you died? You would want to know how they died. I'm already in pain. There is nothing you can tell me that would make this pain any worse," I reassured my parents. They exchanged a look, and I knew that they were conflicted about telling me, but they came this far, so they might as well tell me the rest.

"Luca, Jonah committed suicide. Nikki and—" My father didn't even finish what he said before I ended up punching a hole in the wall.

"Don't lie on my brother, Pops! My brother wouldn't do any weak shit like that, man. I know he had marital problems, but he wouldn't take his life over them. Did that bitch Brii kill him?" I asked. Part of me figured maybe Brii did it and they took the heat off of her so I wouldn't end up killing her ass, but the bitch just wrote her death certificate.

"No! Listen, son. You can't go around blaming people—"

"Then tell me what the fuck happened to Jonah because he isn't a weak nigga. If he really did kill himself as you said, then there was a reason he did it. You better starting before I go painting these streets red looking for answers." I got up off the ground and ran towards my bedroom. I didn't have time to waste kee-keeing with my parents when they didn't want to tell me what was really going on. I was going to find out one way or the other.

"Luca!!! Come here, baby, please!" My mom was chasing after me, but I was much faster than her. However, my father was also chasing me and managed to get inside my room before I could lock the door.

"Luca! I am not about to let you go out there being reckless. Now if you want to know what happened, sit your ass down. I'm going to tell you, but you need to sit your ass somewhere!" My father yelled. His hands were trembling, and his eyes looked like they were blood-shot-red. I felt bad for making my parents upset. I knew none of this was their fault, but I needed to place blame on someone for Jonah's death and the easiest person to blame was Brii.

"What happened, Pops?" All the air just left my body, and I ended up collapsing on my bed. My father opened the door, let my mother in, and she ran to be by my side.

"Jonah got a call from Nikki because she was worried about Brii. Jonah went to his house to check on her, and Nikki and Kobe met them there. Jonah found Brii's body lying on the ground. She had taken a bunch of pills and tried to kill herself. Jonah must have thought she was dead because he shot himself in the head right after that. Nikki and Kobe saw him shoot himself at point blank range and they are devastated. They have their kids and are unsure of what to tell them."

"They need to tell those kids that Brii is a fucking murderer! Jonah's death is Brii's fault, and she better be fucking dead from swallowing those pills or I'm going to finish her ass off! Fuck that scandalous bitch!" I felt like I was losing my damn mind. How could my brother act so weak over Brii's ass? I knew that he was in love with her but hell, if she wasn't acting right, there was plenty of fish in the sea. Jonah lost himself chasing behind a bitch that didn't even appreciate him. Hell, she didn't even want to have kids with him and was selfish enough to think Jonah should just give in to what she wanted. She didn't realize that her actions hurt him.

"Luca, you don't mean it. I know you're upset and you're hurting right now but you are not the only one that is going through it right now."

"Fuck all that. I don't care what anyone else is going through right now. My brother is fucking gone. I will never talk shit with him over sports again or chop shit up with him. Man, this wasn't a random nigga in the streets. This is my fucking brother and I'm just supposed to sit here and take this fucking L? Hell how could Jonah leave me?" I cried, and I couldn't stop crying. I just laid there with my parents listening to me cry until I finally fell asleep.

10

KLAYTON

Luckily, Trayce and Ro agreed to step up to the plate and take temporary custody of Danielle. The doctor came back and said that Danielle had a mild concussion but no brain damage or anything more severe, so I was happy about that.

"Do you guys have any questions for me?" The doctor asked and no one said anything, so he continued speaking. "I will go get Danielle's discharge paperwork ready, and she can go home with you guys. I will recommend that you pick up some children's aspirin in case she has any headaches. If Danielle starts vomiting, coughing up blood or has dizzy spells, you need to bring her back to the emergency room."

I quickly choked the doctor up against the wall. "If there is a risk of all of that happening to my daughter, why is she being discharged, you fucking goofy looking quack? I do not fucking play about my daughter, and I will—"

"Klayton, stop! Let the doctor go!" Trayce ordered and managed to lessen my grip on the doctor's neck. Ro was used to my antics, and she knew that I wasn't working with a full deck as it was. Sparkle looked shocked, and I kicked myself in the foot for being so impulsive. This definitely was not a good look for me, but I was not in a good place right now.

"Umm, I was just warning you in case those things happen. It doesn't mean that they will happen to Danielle but if they do, you need to bring her back to get seen immediately." The doctor looked scared, and rightfully so. If Sparkle wasn't here, I would kill the damn doctor and have no regrets doing it.

Ro quickly intervened. "Forgive Klayton, he is going through a tough time. I understand and will make sure to follow up with her doctor this week. Can you please hurry up with her discharge paperwork?"

The doctor nodded and ran out of the room to get the discharge paperwork done. Sparkle decided she had some shit to say. "Listen, I need to do a home inspection and make sure everything is fit for you guys to keep Danielle. I get good vibes from you guys, but I need to do my job. I need your address and I will follow you guys there."

Trayce looked like he wanted to object, but he thought better of it. "That is fine. Klayton, can you go pick up the children's aspirin for Danielle and Ro and I can go and get the inspection done?" He asked, and I gave him a head nod. The main thing was making sure that my little princess was going to be good.

The next day...

Luckily, everything checked out with the home inspection and my brother was allowed to keep Danielle. Until shit with this Kamar nigga was handled, that was probably the best thing for her anyways right now. I had several missed calls from Treasure, but I had no words for her right now. The worst part of it was I was in love with a woman that could have killed my daughter. Deep down, I knew what happened was an accident, but I wasn't quite ready to forgive her just yet. Luca had sent me several threatening text messages, and I was sick of his ass too. I was trying not to beat his ass, but since Treasure and I weren't together anymore, it really didn't matter. He was about to get this ass whooping he had been asking for. Luca's number popped up on my phone again and this time I answered it.

"What the fuck you want, you fucking bitch ass nigga?" I wasted no time playing with his ass because there was no love lost between us.

"Fuck youuuuu, asshole," Luca slurred. He sounded like he was fucking drunk and I was disgusted by him. He really needed to get help and get himself together for Treasure's sake. He was single-handedly ruining his family and he didn't even see that.

"Nigga, if you want to hash this shit out then let's do this in person. If your punk ass wants to fight, we can fucking do that too. Hell, you know where the fuck I live. I will leave the fucking gate open for your ass."

"Fuck you, Klayton. You have to have every fucking bitch that I got. First, you were fucking AJ, and now you let my ex-girlfriend suck your dick. I knew you were never going to be good enough for Treasure, and I'm going to kill you. Mark my words—" Luca slurred.

"Nigga, be about it instead of making a fucking threat. I promise you this isn't what the fuck you want. I'm not pressed for your women. Wait? That Gigi chick was your girlfriend? Hell, maybe your dick game isn't on point because the night we were at the club, she was acting single as fuck. I didn't know she was connected to you."

"Fuck you! You always have to take what the fuck in mine. You're about to see me!" Luca yelled and hung up on me.

I had a few questions in my head after that conversation. I walked over to the mini bar that I had in my cabinet and pulled out a full bottle of Henny before taking a sip. Did Gigi know about my connection to Luca? Could she have been at the club that night on some scandalous plotting shit? Deep down, something told me she didn't know, the same way that I didn't because I didn't get any negative vibes from her. However, I knew more than anyone that not everyone can be trusted, especially someone with a big butt and a smile.

I finished downing a few shots and sat down deep in thought. I never meant to hurt Treasure the way that I did, but I obviously hurt her, and I couldn't apologize enough for what happened. I shouldn't have put myself in the position to get blackmailed and Danielle never would have gotten hurt. I also blamed Treasure for being reckless and irresponsible. She knew that my child was in the house and while we didn't know that she was in the room, Treasure shouldn't have had that gun out while she was in an emotional state.

I could have handled her thinking that she was gonna leave a real nigga and even trying to leave, but to put my daughter in danger was something that I couldn't easily forgive even if I wanted to. The problem was, my heart beats for Treasure and I miss her so much, but I also knew that we needed time apart. I needed to explain my side of the story and what really happened, but how do you explain letting some bitch blow your mic while her ass was in a fucking coma? I knew I was wrong, but I felt like what Treasure did was worse because my child could have died as a result of her actions.

There was a loud knock on my front door, and it startled me. I had a feeling it was Luca because I left my gate open just like I said I would. If he felt like jumping froggy, we could get it. I went and grabbed one of my guns and went strapped. I wasn't trying to use my gun, but I knew better than to chance getting caught slipping since I had an enemy out there lurking. I opened it and saw a drunk Luca standing there. He saw me and threw a punch that fucking missed and got nothing but air.

"You are a sorry ass piece of shit for breaking my sister's heart. I'm going to kill your ass and eventually, she will understand I'm only doing what is best for her because you are no good for her. You can't even keep your dick in your pants while she is in a fucking coma." Luca pointed his finger at me, and it was war.

I shouldn't have considered fighting Luca knowing that he was drunk, but I had enough of his disrespect. There were only so many times that I was going to continue turning the other cheek when he kept throwing the past in my face. I quickly knocked his ass out with a two-piece combo, and his body fell to the floor. Satisfied with the damage that I did, I was about to leave Luca's ass on the ground, but I was startled to see Giovanni and Hope running inside.

Giovanni shook his head and bent over to pick up Luca, which wasn't an easy task, but Giovanni was hanging tough on his own. "I knew his ass was going to come over here on some reckless shit. Klayton, you knew damn well Luca is drunk, so why would you even fight his ass?"

"No disrespect, Giovanni, but Luca has been asking for this ass whooping for a while. I let him put his hands on me twice and didn't fight back. He has been leaving me threatening text messages and I'm already sick of his shit. My daughter just got out of the hospital. I don't have any patience for his shit." I didn't give a fuck about Luca being drunk. He came over here on that same bullshit energy, so he could take that knockout that he deserved.

"Hope, I'm going to put him in our car. Can you drive Luca's car back to the house? I'm going to bring Luca back in a few minutes, but I want to talk to Klayton for a second," Giovanni ordered.

"Listen nigga. You're not gonna bark orders at me like I'm a dog. Go get Luca in the car, so I can talk to Klayton real quick," Hope bossed up on Giovanni and from the way Hope just looked at me, I knew this conversation wasn't going to be nice.

Giovanni shook his head and continued struggling to get Luca's unconscious body out of the house. "Come with me in the kitchen, Hope."

I dreaded talking to her because I didn't know if Treasure told her anything. I walked to the refrigerator, grabbed a bottle of juice and three glasses and poured everyone, except Luca, a cup. I knew Giovanni would be back in a minute to join the conversation. I handed Hope her cup and for some reason, she had me shook more than Kamar and Luca put together.

"Klayton, I like you, but you got me fucked up." Hope pointed her finger at me, and I was shocked. I never saw the hood in her come out, but I admired it because I knew she was only here to defend her daughter.

"What is your point?" I asked coldly. I didn't hold her going to war for Treasure against her, but the only person I could give a real fuck about right now is Danielle. She is the true victim in all of this drama.

"You broke my daughter's heart and that isn't something I take lightly."

"Don't you think I am paying enough for what happened? Yes, I fucked up and I take responsibility for the club incident, but she could have killed my daughter, Hope. That trumps anything you are trying to say to me right now. Thankfully Danielle is ok, but CPS took my own child from me because of the incident. So believe me, I'm getting my own dish of karma behind it. What I did wasn't right, but I also wasn't thinking straight when Treasure was in that coma. One of my friends invited me out to go to the club because I had been depressed, and I made a bad decision," I explained. I really didn't owe Hope an explanation, but I chose to give her one because she had been nothing but kind to me since I started seeing Treasure.

Hope grabbed my hand and squeezed it. "Listen, I know you are human, and we all make mistakes. I know that you didn't mean for things to happen the way you did, but you can't use your dick as a coping mechanism."

"Trust me, with the old Klayton, that would be true because I was fucking women in different area codes: 323, 424, 919, shit, even 917 area codes up in New York because I had it like that. I started slowing my hoeish ways down even before Treasure came back into my life because I have a daughter, and I have to be an example for her. I might have had one or two broads I was blessing with this pipe, but that wasn't on the daily like I used to. I'm not the same man that I used to be, and I'm sick of having to prove myself to everyone. I messed up, I made a mistake and I take responsibility for that, but my past will not continue to be thrown in my face," I checked Hope.

"Hey, don't talk to my wife like that. I will kill your ass behind Hope and Treasure. Now, what did I tell you when we first talked about you and Treasure? You agreed you wouldn't do any fuck shit to break her heart. You will prove yourself as much as you need to prove yourself because as of right now, my daughter is sitting there with a broken heart." Giovanni got in my personal space. I stood up and we were chest bumping almost.

There was no way I was going to let another nigga check me in my own damn house. I don't fear any nigga. He bleeds out the same way that I do. "The way I see it, Treasure and I are even. Did she even tell you she could have killed my daughter? She was acting reckless, threatening to shoot me, and Danielle could have died. Luckily, she wasn't hit by the bullet and only has a concussion from falling because the sound of the gun going off scared her. I more than paid for what I did, and Treasure needs to take responsibility for what she did wrong. I love her and will apologize for hurting her, but I'm also not kissing her ass. My name is Klayton motherfucking Jackson and nursing Treasure's hurt feelings is simply not my focus right now."

Giovanni looked pissed and if looks could kill, I would be dead. I also noticed that he had a glimmer of respect for me in his eyes. I would never back down from the next person. I would keep it real. And if he accepted my explanation, then he did. If he didn't, that's fine too, but the only people I owed an apology to are Treasure and Danielle for putting her in harm's way.

"I know that you love her, Klayton. I can see it in your eyes, and I apologize for what happened to your child. I wouldn't wish that even on my worst enemy. Maybe you guys need time apart because right now your actions are proving Luca right. I'm not happy about you hitting Luca, but I also know it was well overdue with all of the bull-shit that he has been on. How is Danielle doing?" Giovanni asked.

The tension in the room was slowly lifting, and I think we were all able to relate as parents. I felt for them because of all that Luca was putting them through. At the end of the day, that was still their child. "First, let me say this. If Luca was any other nigga off of the streets, I would have been had him killed, but I haven't out of respect for your family. You are really going to have to get Luca under control. I don't know how much longer I'm going to be able to keep myself from murking his ass. Danielle is resting comfortably at my brother's house. Thankfully, CPS agreed to let my brother take temporary custody of her."

"Klayton, I know Treasure was wrong and I made sure I talked to her, but I really want you guys to work it out. You both need some time and if it is meant to be, you guys will find your way back to each other."

11

TREASURE

A *few days later...*

Shit has been crazy lately. I heard that Luca drove to Klayton's house drunk and acted an entire ass. I was embarrassed. I knew that he was grieving Jonah's death, but he had been acting like a fuck boy for a while now, and I was tired of giving him passes. I wanted to be there for him but every time I tried to go to his house and visit him, he would either not let me in the house or if he did answer, he would say he can't rock with me because I fuck with the enemy now. I refused to let my brother make me feel guilty for following my heart.

I was sitting at Jonah's funeral and I was heartbroken and grieving as well. He was an amazing big brother. If there were things that I didn't feel comfortable talking to Luca about, I could always talk to him. I was sad because Brii had been transferred to a mental hospital, and she wasn't allowed to attend Jonah's funeral. I went out with Ro and Nikki last night, and we had caught up on all of the drama that had been going on with each other. Once I learned the full circumstances of Jonah's death, my mouth had dropped. Part of me felt bad for Brii, but part of me was disgusted because I felt like she was being selfish.

The preacher had finally finished his long sermon about Jonah being in a better place, and I had been in tears the entire funeral. Luca was sitting in the front row stone-faced with a bottle of alcohol in his hand. My mom had been staying with him the last few days, and I could tell she was exhausted and having a hard time. Pops had been helping Genesis and I get settled in their new house. I vowed that soon I would get my shit together and get my own place for Genesis and me. It was a closed casket funeral and it was sad because we couldn't even see Jonah's body to get any sort of closure.

"Jonah, my nigga, you can't be gone. We were supposed to grow old together!" Luca started sobbing and it broke my heart. No matter what differences we had, that was still my brother, and I wanted to be there for him.

I got up and went to put my arms around my brother. I noticed my mom was trying to pry the Jack Daniels bottle of out Luca's hand. The second I touched Luca, he looked up and stared at me. I saw nothing but hatred in his eyes. I took a couple of steps back and was taken aback by his reaction to me. He was looking at me like I was one of these random bitches in the streets.

"Luca, I love you. Let me be here for you." I tried hugging him again, and Luca moved away from me.

"Get away from me, you evil bitch. I don't have a sister anymore since you decided to fuck with the enemy! Fuck you and fuck Genesis too!" Luca's drunk ass slurred. Time stood still and I froze in disbelief at the words that came out of his mouth. Luca has done and said some foul shit, but this was low even for him.

"Nigga, you said fuck me and fuck my daughter? Fuck you, Luca!" I screamed, and I started beating on him in the middle of the damn funeral. I didn't care who was watching this spectacle now because he needed his ass whooped. I could hear my mom and dad in the background, but I started to lose control of myself, and I completely spazzed on my brother. I started biting him and throwing punches. I didn't even care if the punches landed. I could hear one of the voices in my head telling me to wild the fuck out and beat his ass in front of everyone. I finally felt a pair of strong arms pull me away from Luca, and I felt myself visibly relax. I knew that smell anywhere. I knew it was Klayton. My first thought was what was he doing at Jonah's funeral? I should be mad at him, but I forgot why I was mad at him.

"Treasure, stop it! I will drag your ass out of here!" Klayton warned, and I could feel my lady parts getting wet. There was nothing like a nigga in charge and Klayton was definitely running shit with me, but I couldn't let myself be weak over his ass.

"Fuck you, Klayton, with your dirty dick ass. Put me down!" I ordered. I should have known that he wasn't going to listen. He threw me over his shoulder and carried me out bridal style, walking out of the funeral. I was kicking and screaming. He threw me in the back seat of his car then entered the driver's side and locked the doors.

"I wouldn't try to get out of the car because I got the safety locks on," Klayton replied casually like his behavior was fucking normal. He put his seatbelt on and then started driving away. I had no idea where we were going.

"I should call the fucking police on your ass for kidnapping me, Klayton. For all I know, you're about to kill me and—"

Klayton quickly pressed on the breaks and stopped the car in the middle of fucking traffic. He got out of the car and cars were honking. He pulled his gun out and started shooting bullets in the air. "Shut the fuck up! A nigga has to handle some shit real quick!"

"Are you fucking crazy? You are asking for twelve to lock your reckless ass up, Klayton!" I screamed. No matter how mad at him I was, the fact of the matter remained that I am madly in love with this man. I didn't want him to end up in prison or dead regardless if we worked things out or not.

"You should apologize to all these motherfuckers who can't go anywhere, Treasure. It is your fault that my ass stopped traffic. See what happens when you threaten a real fucking nigga." Klayton had an almost sinister grin on his face, and I knew then not to get on his bad side again.

"Klayton, I'm sorry. Let's go, and we can talk about this when we get to where ever we are going. Calm down," I tried reasoning with him, and I finally saw his eyes start to soften.

"Don't ever threaten to call the pigs on my ass again, Treasure, or your parents might end up burying your ass next. It isn't a threat. I'm making a promise." Klayton reached over and kissed me on the lips before closing my door, getting back in on the driver's side and driving away. Part of me wanted to ask him where we were going, but I was too afraid to even ask him. I refused to say a word to him because I wanted to stay mad at him, remember that he is not good for me, and I needed to keep my distance.

He kept driving until he finally pulled back up to the house I just left recently. I don't know what Klayton thought this was, but he does not run shit with me. I sat there in my skin. Once he got in the house, my ass was going to run and call an Uber, but Klayton already sensed I was on bullshit.

"I suggest your childish ass goes in the house if you know what is good for you. You will have your blood on your hands and the Uber driver's blood on your hands too." Klayton unlocked the doors and got out of the car.

"Nigga, I fucking hate you! I wish you would leave me alone!" I cried, frustrated at everything that had been happening lately. I was upset that Danielle was hurt because of our drama, the situation with Luca, and I was in love with a man that obviously wasn't any good for me. I was also worried about Genesis and the possibility of her getting the eye surgery that she needed.

"You know you don't mean that. I know you are mad at me because I fucked up, but I know you don't hate me. You love me as much as I love you. Now stop playing with a nigga and get your ass in the house," Klayton ordered and went inside the house. Hell, the least he could have done was open the damn door for me. I finally walked inside and saw Klayton smoking a blunt. He looked stressed out, and I felt kind of bad because I should have asked him how Danielle was doing instead of getting on his nerves.

"Why do you want me here, Klayton? Things obviously aren't good between us and—"

"I saw you wilding out at the funeral, and I had to make sure you were good. I'm mad at you for how you handled our situation, but I care about you too much to leave you out there looking goofy. I know the gun incident was an accident, but CPS took Danielle away from me," Klayton admitted and my heart went out to him.

Klayton was a lot of things, and he certainly did mess up, but he didn't deserve to lose his daughter because of that. I certainly could have handled things differently, and I knew I needed to apologize. It pissed me off though because if Klayton never let that hoe suck his dick in the club, that incident would have been avoided.

"Listen Klayton. I'm sorry for my role in the incident. I was emotional and lost it when I got that text message. It hurt me to know that when I was in a coma, you let another woman sample what was supposed to be mine. I'd been defending you to Luca, and I feel like you proved Luca right when you fucked up," I admitted and felt tears slide down my cheeks. My hands were shaking because my mind started going back to when I opened that text message. I was also scared to tell Klayton that Luca triggered my schizophrenia, which was why I acted the way I did at the funeral. Deep down, I knew that he would understand, but there is still such a big stigma with mental illness, and I was scared.

"I understand you being emotional, and I'm sorry that I failed you, Treasure. When you were laid up in a coma, I blamed myself for you getting hurt, and I made bad decisions. I never should have gone to the club with Derek that night knowing that I was in a vulnerable state emotionally. The next thing I knew, I was in the bathroom letting her suck my dick, and I immediately regretted it." Klayton had finished smoking his blunt and pulled out a bottle of Hennessey.

I got up and grabbed the bottle out of his hand. "That alcohol is not going to make you feel better, trust me. It might work temporarily, but you will still have the same problems that you had before. Klayton, I'm mad at you, but I never blamed you for me getting hurt. You had no way to know that was going to happen because I know you would have had me out of harm's way. I love you, but that was not an excuse to let her suck your dick. Did you know that was Luca's girlfriend?" I had to ask because Klayton did not have the best track record, and it would make sense that he would do that to get back at Luca. I was conflicted because I didn't know what to believe.

"As a man, it is always my job to protect you, even from things that I don't know about. I'm supposed to be your Superman, and I failed you, Treasure, in more ways than one. I can't forgive myself for that. I saw you at the funeral wilding out, and I had to look out for you. I heard what Luca said and that was fucked up. I figured even though we are going through some and we are both fucked up emotionally, we can really help each other." Klayton shrugged his shoulders.

"It almost broke me to hear Luca say fuck me and fuck Genesis. It is the worst thing I have heard him say in a long while. What scares me is I don't know if my brother will ever really be the same again, and I miss my brother. I miss when Luca and I used to be close. However, he won't fuck with me now because he feels like I'm disloyal to him. I just want to be happy, Klayton," I whispered, trying to keep myself from crying.

Klayton and I have issues that we have to work through, but at the end of the day, he is my best friend and I can tell him anything. I was trying to stay strong in front of Klayton, but I knew that was over with when I felt him wrap his big arms around me. "Treasure, I think that we need to get away from all of the drama we are dealing with in LA, even if just for a weekend. What do you think about taking a trip to Las Vegas?"

I have never been to Vegas, so I looked forward to gambling for the first time and getting away from all of my problems. "I don't want you to think that I am agreeing to get back together with you."

"Who said anything about that? Besides, you know if you even entertain another nigga, you will have his blood on your hands. I will kill him and his entire fucking family. We might not be on good terms right now, but don't play with me, Treasure," Klayton warned and my lady parts started throbbing again.

"As long as you know I'm going to fight any bitch that looks at your ass, Klayton. You made my ass crazy," I warned him. I ended up looking down and could see his dick was hard as a rock in his pants. I was drooling at the thought of finally having sex with Klayton even though I knew that wasn't going down right now.

"You see something you like, Treasure?" Klayton smirked and I blushed.

"Nigga you must see something you like because your dick is about to bust out of your pants. When are we leaving for Vegas?"

12

BRII

It was bad enough that I had been transferred to a mental health facility called Sunny dale. But to have to cope with the fact that Jonah truly was dead was eating me alive. My selfish actions cost me the love of my life and the kids the only stability that they've ever really known. What made it worse was that no one came to visit me after the incident with Nikki and Kobe, and I felt like I was the black sheep of the crew. Every day I woke up, I wished I was dead. I really felt like I had nothing to live for. Hell, the kids would be better off with Nikki and Kobe anyways, but I couldn't do anything while I was admitted to this fucking facility.

"Brii, how are you doing today?" Stephanie, one of my many therapists, asked me.

"How the fuck do you feel like I'm doing?" I asked sarcastically.

"It sounds like you are frustrated, and you are displacing your frustration on me. What is on your mind?" Stephanie asked patiently.

"I want to get the fuck out of here, is what the fuck is wrong with me! I don't see why I need to be here." I started tapping my foot on the ground impatiently.

"I know it isn't the most ideal situation being hospitalized involuntarily, Brii. We are all here to help you. Once we are confident that you are doing better, you will be able to go home. However, the longer you try to fight counseling and say nothing during sessions, the longer you will be here. I cannot clear you to go home when I know that there is plenty of work that we need to do," Stephanie replied. She grabbed her coffee cup and took a sip of her coffee.

"If you know it all, then why don't you tell me what I need to do to get better? You seem to know more about my own life than I do," I pointed out sarcastically.

Honestly, Stephanie has had the patience of a saint because I either have been saying nothing during sessions or I have been yelling at her for no reason. I was angry at my counselor, but I wasn't sure why I resented her. Maybe it was because she represented someone that had the perfect life, and I was stuck in a situation where I had to live a life that was completely fucked up.

"I don't know anything about your life other than what is in your file, and that doesn't tell me much of anything, Brinisha. I prefer to get to know my clients personally and hear your story from you personally. There is so much that we can teach each other, but I can't help you unless you allow me to help you." Stephanie was slowly but surely starting to break down my walls. I was getting tired of living life in survival mode and being wary of who to trust.

"You want to know what my story is? My story is I never got to really live my childhood because my twin sister and I were stuck raising our siblings since our mother was a fucking crackhead. Then when things started to look like they were getting better for AJ and me, AJ ended up getting shot and died. That left me with the responsibility to raise my brother and sister. Don't get me wrong, I love Antoinette and Blake. I would give my life for them with no questions asked, but I never got to live life and be selfish. I have goals and dreams that I never got to pursue." I paused and sat in deep thought.

"You lived a very hard life, Brii, but let me tell you that I admire your strength. It takes a strong woman to overcome everything that you have faced, especially losing your twin sister. How did you get through that tough period in your life? There had to have been some things that helped you cope when you lost your sister. I want to figure out what resources you had that we can utilize to help you regain the strength that you had."

"Honestly, I don't know if I was ever strong because I feel like I hid how I was really feeling. I did my best to grieve her death and now it is three years later, and I still don't feel like I really healed from her death. When you lose someone that close to you, I don't know if you ever really get over it. I had to stay strong for the sake of Antoinette, Blake, Leslie and my husband, Jonah, and it took a toll on me over the years," I explained, and I felt guilty. Maybe if I had communicated better with Jonah about why I didn't want to have kids, we wouldn't be in the place that we were now. The thing with life is you don't get do-overs. You can't erase what happens in life like you would delete a video recording.

"As women, we tend to wear different hats and roles. It is hard for us in society to figure out our own identity while raising children and making sure we are taking care of our significant other. I can understand why you felt the need to wear a mask, Brii, because you felt like you couldn't put your needs first," Stephanie explained. It felt like a lightbulb was starting to go off in my head.

"I really couldn't. My entire life I have had to consider what was best for everyone, and I think it contributed to the demise of my marriage. See, Jonah wanted to have biological kids with me, but I never wanted kids. I spent most of my life raising my siblings, and I couldn't really get with the idea of having kids that I would have to raise from birth. Granted, it was selfish because my husband stepped up to the plate to help me raise my siblings and find them when they were missing, and he really never asked too much from me. I had been feeling bad lately because the one thing that he wants was something that I simply wasn't willing to give him. I felt like this was my one chance to be selfish and think about what Brii wants."

"Did you and Jonah ever discuss having kids? That is something you guys should have discussed before getting married." Stephanie took a sip of her drink.

"Honestly, no we didn't. We fell in love quickly and it was weird because we were engaged for a year. We never talked about those things that we should have talked about because I would have made it clear that I wasn't having any kids. I feel like I lost my childhood due to raising my siblings. I wanted to live life and do something for Brii. I still want to start my own business and travel around the world. We already had Leslie, who was someone we rescued from a bad situation and my siblings, so I figured he knew that those three would be enough," I explained my logic although, now I was seeing that I shouldn't have assumed anything.

"Here is a question. Why couldn't you start a business, travel and have children of your own? I'm not saying that you had to have your own kids considering society judges people that choose to be childless, but it seems like you were close-minded about even considering the idea."

"I know that I could have, and Jonah would have been a great help, so I wouldn't be raising the kids on my own, but it was just something that I was unwilling to consider. I love him and he could have asked me for anything else. Hell, he could have asked for a threesome with another woman. I was more likely to give him that than to give him a child of his own," I admitted. Granted, I was damaged by my past, but I was just starting to realize the extent of the hurt I was feeling.

"It sounds like you are not only dealing with grieving AJ, but you still have issues that go back to your childhood. I would like to help you work through those if you allow me to help you." Stephanie reached out and held my hand.

I was touched by her gesture, but the question remained. Did I really want help? I knew that I needed to find the strength for myself first and then for the kids, but I also knew that Nikki would give me a hard time about getting them back when I was done with treatment. "I don't know if I'm worth saving, Stephanie. Honestly, the kids are in a much better place now—"

"What do you mean by that?" Stephanie interrupted me.

"The kids are with my former friend named Nikki. The last time I saw her was right after my suicide attempt. She came into my hospital room calling me selfish, and she also said I would never see the kids again. Those words almost broke me down again," I admitted.

"I'm sure she just felt hurt and maybe she didn't mean what she said. Sometimes people say things out of anger, and they don't always understand suicide and depression. They might view it as selfish when, in reality, you are only looking at what you feel like is your only option," Stephanie tried reassuring me.

"Nikki seemed very angry. I don't think she is going to change her mind anytime soon. The thing is, I can't blame her because I understand why she feels that way." I was struggling with whether I could really tell Stephanie why Nikki was so angry at me. At the end of the day, Jonah's blood was on my hands, and I also knew that Nikki and Kobe were scarred for life.

"Are you ready to talk about it or is this something that you would feel better talking about next session? I know that we have made good progress today, and I don't want to push you too far." Stephanie looked concerned.

Part of me was grateful to have a reprieve, but I also knew that I needed to finish telling her my truth. "No, I need to get this out while I'm brave enough to tell you. When I overdosed on pills, my husband found my body, and he was devastated. He ended up shooting himself in the head in front of Nikki and Kobe, and that is why I think I will never get custody of the kids again."

13

GIOVANNI

Things have already been going bad, but it got even worse when Treasure and Luca got into it at Jonah's funeral. It was tough trying to be the strong one in the family, especially since I didn't know if things would ever be fixed between Treasure and Luca. The things he said to his sister were foul as hell, and he was going to have to hear from me now that the funeral was over. I wasn't too pressed about Treasure, only because I knew Klayton would make sure she was safe. Hope and I were focused on getting Luca's drunk ass out to the family car when gunshots started going off.

Pow! Pow! Blocka! Blocka!

"Hope, get down!" I yelled and pushed Luca down to the ground, but it was too late. He was hit by a stray bullet in the stomach. I knew I had to hurry and get him to the hospital.

Gunshots were flying in different directions. I didn't even have time to reach for my fucking strap. Kamar's ass must have struck knowing that Klayton was here. I had to pray that Luca would be ok temporarily because I couldn't move him until the gunshots stopped. Derek and Trouble were busting their guns back in the direction where the gunshots were coming from until the sound of gunfire ceased. They ran up on us to assist me with Luca.

"We got to get him to the fucking hospital!" Derek yelled, and he helped me carry Luca to the car. Thankfully, Nikki and Kobe agreed to watch Genesis, so she wasn't here. Hope ran and got in on the passenger side. I got in the driver's seat and started driving like a bat out of hell.

"Hope, are you ok?" I asked frantically. I didn't even have time to really check to see if she got hit by a bullet because I was worried about getting to the emergency room before Luca bled out. I wasn't much of a praying man, but I had to pray that Luca would be ok. Maybe this would be the wake-up call that he needed to get help.

"I'm good, Gio. Please let Luca survive!" Hope cried. I wanted to comfort her but now was not the time for me to get soft.

"I need you to be strong right now, Hope. We are going to speak positivity into existence," I coached her and finally pulled up to the emergency room.

"Let me run and get someone to bring a gurney out," Hope ran out the car. I prayed they hurried up because it looked like Luca might bleed out.

Luckily, I saw Hope come out with a couple of medical personnel and a gurney. I got out of the car to help them get Luca's body on the gurney. "Please save my son. I can't bear losing him," I begged.

"We will do everything we can to save him, I promise." They looked sympathetic. We finally got him strapped on the gurney and they rushed his body inside to start working on him.

"We need to call Klayton and Treasure and let them know Luca got shot," Hope insisted. I knew that she was right, especially because we shouldn't keep any more secrets from Treasure, but I already knew Luca wasn't her favorite person right now. I couldn't say that I blamed her, but family needs to stick together during hard times, and I know that she would want to be here.

"Go fill out the medical paperwork for Luca, and I will call Klayton and give him the news. I love you, Hope." Life is too short to not tell the people you love that you love them.

"I love you too, Gio. I will be right in the waiting room if you need me. Don't take too long," Hope went inside the hospital. I appreciate how she is my backbone, and she knows when to not give me a hard time. Don't get me wrong, she isn't a weak woman, but she knows when to listen to me and let me be the man.

I grabbed my phone, dialed Treasure's number first and listened to it go to voicemail. I decided to leave a message for her. "Listen Treasure. I know that you are with Klayton. We were leaving the funeral and it got shot up. I need you to tell Klayton to call me. Your brother got shot in the stomach, and he is in the emergency room. I need you to get to Little Company of Mary as soon as possible. I love you, Treasure, and we will get through this as a family."

I hung up the phone and dialed Klayton's number. He didn't answer, but I kept trying. I was desperate to get ahold of him. He should have known by now that this was an emergency. Thankfully, he finally answered the phone.

"What's up, Giovanni?" Klayton asked curiously.

"Listen, not long after you and Treasure left, the funeral got shot up and Luca is in the emergency room. He was shot in the stomach, and we are at Little Company of Mary's." I didn't want to say too much over the phone because the FEDS could be listening.

"Say less. I will bring Treasure up there and see you in a little bit." Klayton hung up. I walked back inside the emergency room. I was deep in thought. When it rains, it pours, but when would it stop raining on the Glover family?

I walked inside and saw Hope sitting in a chair with her head in her hands. I knew she was stressed out and it was my job to make things better. "Babe, Luca is going to be ok. I promise you."

"We don't know that, Gio. What if Luca doesn't make it? He was bleeding everywhere," Hope cried.

"You're right. We don't know that Luca is going to be ok, but we are going to speak positivity into existence. When we are given a bunch of lemons, we must make lemonade with them. We gotta stay strong right now." I held Hope in my arms. There wasn't a more helpless feeling in the world than to know that you might have to bury your child. I don't know if it was worse knowing Luca might not make it through this or knowing that Luca hasn't really been himself for the last three years. Hope was about to respond, but Klayton and Treasure walked in the living room.

"How is Luca doing?" Treasure asked. One thing about my daughter, she has a big heart. Even though Luca had been treating her like shit, she was still here to support her brother.

"We don't know. We're waiting for an update on his condition," Hope whispered. Treasure ran and hugged her mom. They both cried. I felt helpless to protect my family.

"Giovanni, let me spit at you for a second," Klayton ordered and I looked over at Treasure and Hope.

"Go ahead, dad. I will be here with mom," Treasure reassured me. I followed Klayton outside.

"What's up, Klayton? I'm glad you took Treasure from the funeral because that could have been my daughter that was shot up." I was feeling emotional. I wish that all of the drama would end.

"It was nothing. I might be mad at her, but I love her more than life itself. It broke my heart to see her breaking down like that. I promise you on God I will protect her with my life," Klayton vowed, and I could see nothing but love in his eyes. I could do nothing but respect that. Klayton messed up, but no one is perfect.

"Just don't break her heart, Klayton. Treasure has been through too much, and she deserves to be happy. I am worried that Luca and Treasure will never fix their fractured relationship," I admitted.

"I will try to talk to her because family is all that we have. I don't like Luca, but I would never encourage Treasure to not have a relationship with him. At the end of the day, that is still her brother. I do plan to take her out of town this weekend to Las Vegas. We both need time away from this drama, but with Luca in the hospital, I'm not sure Treasure will want to go."

"Get her out of here, Klayton. Have you made any headway on finding Kamar?" I asked.

Klayton was about to respond but someone tapped me on the arm. "Excuse me. I couldn't help but overhear part of your conversation. I know the Kamar that you just asked about, and I'm interested in helping you find him." The mysterious female was batting her eyes at Klayton flirtatiously.

"Hoe, who the fuck are you? I don't like bitches that look like the orange cheeto and smell like fucking dollar tree perfume, so stop sniffing at my dick. I would never bless your crazy ass with this good pipe. For all I know, you could be setting me up with Kamar's ass. Why should I trust you?" Klayton asked suspiciously.

"My name is Bethany and trust me, I would never set you up because I value my life. Let me say that I know Kamar personally. He brought me out to Cali with him to be his personal whore. He didn't value me and cheated on me with this fat bitch named Brii, and I let that slide. Hell, I know for a fact that he date raped the bitch and has been obsessed with her ever since, but she has disappeared into thin air. I can help you find him."

Klayton looked around. Thankfully there was no one outside and he grabbed Bethany by her neck. "Listen bitch, you are going to stop talking out of the side of your neck. How the hell do I know that you are not trying to play both sides?"

"Klayton, let her go so she can respond. You're choking the bitch to death." I tapped Klayton on the shoulder, and he reluctantly threw her down on the ground. Her face had turned blue and Bethany started coughing. She looked terrified. She should be, she was playing a very dangerous game.

"Listen Klayton, your name rings bells in LA, and I know you are nothing to play with. The fact remains that Kamar played my ass. He thought he was going to use me and get away with it. I can be a very useful part of the team, if you get my drift," Bethany's nasty ass smiled.

"If you know I'm nothing to play with, stop throwing that fish market pussy at me. I'm in love with someone, and I definitely wouldn't fuck with Kamar's sloppy seconds. The fact remains you are a scorned bitch because you're mad he isn't fucking with you anymore. Giovanni, look out for me real quick." Klayton looked around real quick, grabbed Bethany by the neck and walked towards his car. I watched him throw her ass in the trunk. It was reckless considering it was broad daylight out.

Klayton walked back over casually as if he had just discarded a random piece of trash. "Klayton are you fucking crazy? There could have been police in the area, and you have Treasure with you," I fussed. I understand how the streets work, but I needed Klayton to be more calculated about his moves, especially since my daughter was involved.

"Yo' I'm good and Treasure is going to be good. Yes, I was reckless, but letting her walk would have been reckless in case she was plotting. I plan to drop her ass at the warehouse after dropping Treasure off at Trayce's house. I'm going to tie her ass up until Kamar is found and pick her brain about any useful information that she might have. Either way, she is going to disappear, if you get my drift." Klayton definitely was not working with a full deck of cards.

"I'm going to meet you at the warehouse once I drop Hope off just for backup. We need to keep Bethany around as bait, and I don't want to chance you killing her ass or end up in a bad position dealing with the bitch. These hoes out here are scandalous as you know. Let's go see if there is any news on Luca's condition."

14

GIGI

My ego was bruised that I hadn't heard from Luca lately. Part of me assumed that he would chase after me once he figured out that he was wrong, but that was far from the truth. I haven't heard a peep out of him, and I was a bit insecure. I wasn't used to feeling this way because I never put a lot of energy into relationships with any man. After James broke my heart, I closed myself off to men emotionally, at least until I met Luca. Now I'm madly in love with a man that is probably still in love with AJ's ghost. I understand they had a past together and I would never try to replace her, but I also couldn't live as a replacement either. In all fairness, I couldn't blame all of this on James because Marina's dysfunctional relationship contributed to my mentality on niggas. In my eyes, it was easier for me to hurt Luca than to sit there and wait for him to hurt me.

I finally got a new apartment and went back and got my things. I had paid first month's rent, last month's rent and my security deposit, so the landlord allowed me to move in immediately. Candice and Marina were helping me move in, and I was grateful for their help. I was disappointed in Marina for how weak she was behind Anthony, but I would always support her even if I didn't agree with her choices. Between getting my new place, ordering furniture and handling Luca's clients on top of my own, I had been really busy lately. Yet, there was still this void that was missing in my life and that was Luca. I hated feeling like Luca made me weak even though that was not the case. It felt like I was fighting my own inner battle of whether to let Luca in fully or leave him where he is at.

We had just finished decorating my spot and directing people on where my new furniture should go when we agreed to order some pizzas. I had already placed the order on my phone and was waiting for the pizza to arrive because I was hungry as hell. Candice went to the liquor store to get a couple of bottles of wine, and I was at my apartment alone with Marina. It felt good to have my own place that was mine again. I was tired of staying in hotels.

"How does it feel to have your own space again?" Marina asked me.

"Girl, it feels good, but something still feels empty. I miss Luca, but I don't think that he misses me. I haven't heard from him lately, and I'm wondering if something happened. It is unlike him to go ghost knowing that I'm managing his clients for him." I frowned. My women's intuition was going off.

"Don't let your pride make you lose out on finding love, Gigi. You deserve to be happy and I'm proud of you for achieving your own career. Remember, it won't keep you warm at night. It is ok to fall in love and have a long-term relationship. I feel like you keep punishing yourself because of the past," Marina hugged me.

"I love Luca, but I won't compete with a ghost. I know my own worth, and I refuse to live in AJ's shadow. I care about Luca a lot and in a sense, I can relate to him, but he really needs to get help to deal with his past before I can even consider giving him another chance. I'm scared of falling in love, especially seeing how Anthony did you, Marina. I don't want to be weak behind another man," I admitted.

Marina grabbed my hand and squeezed it. "You can't live life in a bubble. Anything can happen at any time, but you can't be afraid to let love in. Luca seems like a different breed of a man than Anthony. I know that I put up with too much disrespect from him, but you are also much stronger than I am."

There was a knock on the door, and I got up to go answer it. I opened it thinking Candice was at the door but was surprised to see Anthony at the door. He pushed his way inside. "Marina, bring your ass back home, bitch, where you belong."

"Oh, hell naw, nigga. You are not forcing your way into my apartment and calling my best friend out of her name. Get the fuck out before I call the police on your ass." I made my way to my purse and grabbed my mace and my phone. I had no problem sending his ass to jail if he didn't get the fuck out of my house. Anthony and I never got along because I never liked how he treated Marina, and I made it known every time I see him that I wasn't fucking with him on any level. If the word fuck boy was in the dictionary, Anthony's picture would be right beside the word in the dictionary.

"I'm not going anywhere until Marina comes with me. She knows what the fuck it is, don't you, bae?" Anthony smirked like his ass was doing something. I wished Luca was here because I knew Anthony would not be acting all big and bad if he was. Anthony loves flexing on those he perceives to be weak and that was why he would never let Marina go. He plays on Marina's love for him and does whatever he fucking wants to do. Even when Marina puts her foot down, it never lasts very long because he wears her down.

"You are trespassing. I tried warning you motherfucker, but I don't play about my best friend or my sister." I decided to dial 911 and didn't notice that Anthony had put a gun to Marina's head. It takes a lot to scare me but seeing my best friend's life in danger was enough to have me in tears. Marina has gone through too much to have her life end this way, but I had to try to stay strong in the moment.

"Put the fucking phone down if you don't want me to press the trigger!" Anthony screamed. His eyes looked borderline psychotic, and you could tell he wasn't all there. I wasn't sure what to do, but I had to do whatever I could do to save Marina's life.

The operator spoke on the other end of the line, but I was almost too shocked to speak. I was stuck in a crossroads because I wasn't sure that I really wanted to call Anthony's bluff. He had the gun pointed at Marina's head, and she was crying. I hung up the phone and decided to take my chances playing things his way. What Anthony doesn't know is that I have a registered gun and I prayed I could get to it in time before he killed my friend. I hung up on the operator and prayed that she was smart enough to send help to my location even though I didn't say anything.

"You don't need to do this to Marina. She doesn't deserve this and if you kill her, it won't end well for you, Anthony. You will end up spending the rest of your life in prison on murder charges because you won't get away with this. This is something that you can't take back." I was trying to talk him off of the fence. I slowly made my way to my purse where I had a registered gun. Thank God, Anthony wasn't really watching what I was doing. He was staring straight at Marina.

"I love you, Marina. My actions might not reflect that, but I do love you. I got that bitch Serena in check, and she won't give us any problems anymore. I need you to understand that I am not perfect, but I love you in my own way. Niggas fuck up all the time, and I shouldn't have stuck my dick in her, but I did, and I can't take that back. I'm begging you to forgive me so we can move forward and be a family again," Anthony was begging, and the gun was starting to shake in his hand. I wasn't sure if I should try to knock it out of his hand or not and chance the gun going off. *Where was Candice at? She should have been back from the liquor store,* was what I was thinking. I grabbed my gun and pointed it at Anthony.

I was about to pull the trigger, but Marina gestured to me not to. "Anthony, I forgave a lot of your bullshit and took you back when you never even deserved forgiveness. I was weak behind you for so long, and I know that it made Gigi have a negative view on love and relationships. Hell, you could have given me fucking AIDS and your response when I gave you the news was you flipped it on me and blamed me for not being the woman you needed in the bedroom. Do you remember that argument? I wasn't giving you enough pussy, so you went out there and got it from your baby mama and other randoms out there. I can forgive you for all that you put me through, Anthony, but what I can't forgive you for is changing my best friend's views on love and relationships. She is too scared to fall in love because she doesn't want to be weak like I was over you. So, for that, I say fuck you, Anthony, and fuck us ever being together. If you want to pull that fucking trigger, then do it and kill me. Just know that you will have to live with my death and what you put me through for the rest of your life."

Tears were sliding down my face and my hands were shaking. I was having a hard time staying focused on getting a clean shot off on Anthony. I never knew Marina blamed herself for how I chose to live my life. I prayed that we would make it out of this situation, and I was quickly learning that life was too short to live with any regrets.

Before Anthony could respond, the sound of gunshots rang out.

Pow! Pow!

Bullets came in different directions and it was all I could do to get low and get on the ground to avoid getting shot. I lifted the gun up to shoot Anthony when I saw his limp body on the ground on top of Marina's body. I didn't know whether to try to get him off of her or what to do next. I had no idea if Marina was dead or alive because Anthony's body was covering hers, and I let out an earth-shattering scream. My woman's intuition told me that my life would never be the same after this. I had a bad feeling that Marina got shot, and I prayed that she would survive even if there was only a slim chance of survival. The next sight that I saw was Candice walking in the room with her gun pointed at Anthony's lifeless body. There was blood all over the carpet in my new apartment. I knew that I would never spend a single night here and would likely have nightmares about this for the rest of my life. Knowing that Candice came in guns blazing was something that I didn't want for her because that is something that stays with you for the rest of your life. We needed to hurry up and call for an ambulance for Marina. Anthony could bleed out on the ground for all that I cared, but Marina was my main priority.

"Rest in hell motherfucker. I will never forgive you for what you put Marina through."

15

KLAYTON

It was a week later, and it had taken me longer than I had planned to take Treasure to Las Vegas because I had been trying to get information from that Bethany bitch. Unfortunately, I think that I had gotten all of the information that I could from her, and she continued trying to suck my damn dick. I hope you guys had more faith in your boy Klayton than to think I would let a bitch whose mouth looks like Alien versus Predator blow my mic. At least with the Gigi bitch, she was official, but this Bethany hoe looked like a bad reject from the movie *Clueless*. Treasure and I had just arrived, and we were staying at the Cosmopolitan on the Las Vegas Strip. It was nothing but luxurious. I hope you guys didn't think a nigga was gonna stay at the Trump hotel and put money into that orange Cheeto's pockets.

"Klayton, this is so nice. You didn't have to—"

"Don't ever tell me what I have to do. You know a nigga is always going to make sure you are good, Treasure. We might not be fucking with each other right now, but we both know what this is, and I'm damn sure not letting another nigga have you."

I pressed my body against Treasure and could feel myself getting hard. The last couple of weeks I had been questioning myself on how

I could be in love with a woman that almost killed my daughter, but I knew that Treasure would have never threatened me with that gun if she knew Danielle was in the room. I also knew she was acting off of emotions and the situation was partly my fault for putting myself in a compromising situation in the first place, but I was still upset at Treasure for going off of her emotions. Treasure tried to get loose, but my big ass had her pinned to the wall.

"Nigga, you lost any say about who gets to have me after getting your dick sucked in a fucking night club while I was in a coma. Let me fucking go!" Treasure yelled and her little fists were doing very little damage against my rock, solid chest.

She was clearly in her feelings, but I knew just how to shut her ass up. I tilted her head to meet mine and slipped my tongue inside of hers. She tried fighting it at first, but I felt her body giving into me. I finally broke the kiss, carried her bridal style to the bedroom and laid her down on the bed. I stared lovingly into Treasure's eyes.

"I am in love with you. Treasure Glover. I fucked up, and I take responsibility for that, but you have no idea how I felt watching you everyday while you were in a coma. A nigga wasn't himself, point, blank, and I was spazzing on niggas. I caught a few reckless bodies from jack boys trying to sell on my corner, and I made a lot of shitty decisions, including letting Gigi suck me off in that club. If I could go back and change what happened that night, I would, but I can't take back what happened. All I can do is apologize, make sure you know that something like that will never happen again, and my word is everything. I know that I don't have the greatest reputation because of my past, but I promise you that I am a changed man, Treasure. This penthouse and the view from it is beautiful, but it has nothing on your natural beauty, Treasure." I cupped her face in my hands.

What Treasure doesn't understand is that I never had to chase behind pussy, especially pussy I never personally stuck my dick in, but Treasure was worth it. Treasure looked conflicted and I felt bad because I could see how bad I hurt her. I truly didn't mean to hurt her, but I made a mistake.

"I knew that the type of lifestyle you lived, you had women

throwing themselves at you. I'm sure you can have any woman you want, and it just hurt me so much to know that while I was fighting for my life, you were out there getting your dick sucked by the next bitch. It hurts even more that I could hear you crying for me, yet you were still out there doing you, Klayton. I have been through too much to let you break my heart."

"I made a mistake and I'm far from perfect, Treasure. If anything, I don't deserve you, but I am begging for your forgiveness. I need you like I need air to breathe and life has been hell without you lately. You are my soulmate and my better half, Treasure. Just promise to give me a chance, Treasure. If you gave me the chance, I would marry you tomorrow if you wanted me to. I don't care about all of the obstacles that are blocking our love because I know that we are meant for each other. I'm begging you to fight for our love because I promise you that it will be worth it. You get me in ways no other woman has been able to understand me, and you don't see me as a come up, but you see the real Klayton that you can build with. I'm not trying to say that I wasn't wrong for what I did, but I think we are even after what happened with Danielle, and I'm still willing to move forward with you, Treasure." I was pouring my heart out and if Treasure didn't see that, I doubt that we would ever be able to make anything work in the future because I wouldn't pour my heart out to her again.

"Your actions instigated the entire incident though, Klayton. If you never let that bitch suck your dick, the accident would have never happened. I was in my feelings and emotional, and I shouldn't have acted as reckless as I did with a gun, but this is really your fault," Treasure pointed her finger at me.

"I am willing to own up that I was wrong and have been apologizing, Treasure, but one thing I won't do is kiss your ass. The fact remains you knew my daughter was in the house even if she was supposed to sleep in her room. It was irresponsible of you to act reckless with a gun. You could have chosen to leave—"

Treasure started laughing. "Nigga, do you fucking hear yourself? Do you really think you would have let me leave? We both know you wouldn't have let me leave the house. You just want the heat taken off of you."

"You haven't listened to a damn thing that I am saying Treasure. I have been apologizing for what I did and owned up to my responsibility for that. Can you say the same about your actions? I get how you found out was fucked up, but you still had a choice in how you reacted to the situation. Man, this is a fucking mistake, and I should have known you are too young and immature to understand when someone is coming at you trying to make things right. I can live with the fact that we don't agree about the situation, but that is where compromise and talking it out comes in. Are you even ready to be in a serious relationship, Treasure?" I had to ask her because she was still acting like a little girl when I needed her to come to me like a grown ass woman. The only way we could move on and grow together is if we both took responsibility for our actions. I didn't even mention the fact I lost custody of my own child because of her reckless actions.

Treasure started crying. I hated hearing her cry, but at the same time, I couldn't coddle and baby her all of the time. I just needed her to grow up and understand we both played a role in what happened. "Klayton, don't use my age as an excuse. You knew my age when we started dating and reconnected. The real question is why are you almost thirty years old still slanging dick?"

"One thing I'm not going to do is continue kissing your ass, Treasure. I have apologized numerous times over and regardless if we work out or not, I'm always going to look out for you. You don't understand how reckless your actions were. My daughter was taken away from me because of what you did and then you are cutting up at Jonah's funeral. Don't get me wrong, Luca was wrong for disrespecting you, which is why I stepped in, but you have to learn how to take more responsibility for your actions. I know that you are hurting, and I'm trying to be there for you, but I feel like you are pushing me away," I admitted.

Treasure just stared at me for a minute before she broke down sobbing. I reached over and held her in my arms. The sight of Treasure crying almost broke me down. She really doesn't understand the effect that she has on me because I wanted to protect her from everyone that hurt her.

"I love you, Klayton. You are the only man that has managed to break through that wall that I have put up and to imagine you as less than perfect almost broke me. I don't blame you for me being in a coma, but what I am struggling with is forgiving you for the club incident. It might have been easier for me to forgive you if I had heard it from you directly instead of finding out in a text message from Kamar—"

"Wait, how do you know it was Kamar that sent the text message?" I asked confused.

"I called the number when I got back to Luca's house. The guy said his name was Kamar, and he was going to play with my pussy—"

"Treasure, I understand we are on bad terms, but if that nigga calls you or tries anything in public, you need to tell me. This is information that you should have told me sooner because his ass has been plotting to take over LA. Think about it, he sent you that picture because he knows you are my weakness, and he is hoping to catch me slipping. When we get back to LA ,you will have security on you at all times and I'm not taking no for an answer," I insisted. I was trying to keep my anger in because I didn't want to scare Treasure. As soon as I got back to LA, I was going to put all focus on finding that Kamar nigga because his ass has to die.

"Klayton, I will be fine. Kamar did what he wanted to do by splitting us up. He really isn't going to come for me." Treasure sounded naive as fuck, especially considering that Luca used to be in the game. I needed her to boss up, recognize that her life was in danger and to stay alert.

"Treasure, are you that delusional? Your brother used to be in the fucking game. You should know by now that Kamar will likely try you just because you have been associated with me. Like I said before, you will have protection with you at all times and that is not negotiable. Get mad if you want to but your safety is important. Do you really want your parents stressed out about you when Luca is in the hospital still because he got shot in the stomach and recovering from surgery? You need to stop being stubborn, Treasure. We are not going to lose you because you don't understand the gravity of the situation," I lectured her.

Treasure rolled her eyes at me. "Fine, nigga. Can you leave me alone now so I can get some damn sleep?"

I was tired of Treasure's attitude and it was starting to rub me the wrong way considering I was only trying to look out for her. I understood that I hurt her, but if I had to be the bad guy for trying to protect her then I would. I got up and grabbed my hotel room key. I needed to get away from Treasure and go have a drink and a blunt to relax, maybe gamble a little bit.

"I will be back in a bit. Don't wait up," I answered shortly. I needed to leave before I felt like choking the shit out of Treasure.

"Nigga, where are you going?" Treasure asked with an attitude in her voice.

I counted to ten before I responded. "I'm going to go have a drink and do some gambling." I made sure to leave, so I didn't hear anything else that came out of her mouth.

I love Treasure more than life itself, but would we ever be able to work things out?

16

TREASURE

I felt bad for blaming Klayton, and I knew I was wrong, but I couldn't help how I felt. Did I need to grow up? As soon as he left, I regretted a lot of what I said to him, and I knew I was going through one of my hot and cold mood swings. Klayton left me alone in this beautiful penthouse suite where we should have been making love and fixing things. Instead, I was stuck on insecurities and fear. I got up and looked out at the view of the mountains and the sky; it gave me a sense of relief momentarily. I want to be with Klayton more than anything in this world, but fear was holding me back. How would he react when I told him about my schizophrenia diagnosis? It's crazy because I am going to school to become a counselor. I knew that my diagnosis didn't define me as a person, but I was still scared to tell Klayton. The reason why was telling Klayton made it more real for me, and I knew he wouldn't judge me. Hell, he would make sure I was taking my medications as prescribed, but I just didn't want to change how he viewed me.

I went inside the bag I had packed and grabbed a bottle with my prescription and a bottle of water from the mini bar in the room. I went inside the bathroom and took the Zyprexa I was prescribed. I had stopped taking my medications over a year ago because I felt like I was fine, and I didn't need it anymore. I needed to get myself together before I lost the best thing that happened to me, which was Klayton. Deep down, I felt like I wasn't good enough for a man like Klayton, especially since he had gotten his dick sucked by Luca's now ex-girlfriend. There was no way he would stay with her knowing she sucked Klayton off, but if I ever ran into her, I was beating her ass on sight for touching what was mine. Granted, she owed me no loyalty and Klayton did, but Klayton's dick is off limits even if we don't get back together. I also felt guilty for what happened to Danielle, and I had been flipping the guilt I had been feeling on Klayton. Hell, I didn't even understand why he still wanted to be with me because I really could have killed or severely hurt Danielle, and that was never my intention. Then, to find out Danielle was taken from his custody made me feel guilty as hell, so I had been trying to push Klayton away. But for some reason, we kept running back to each other. Then, add on how bad Luca made me feel for falling in love and following my heart. That made me lash out at Klayton too because my relationship with my big brother has been strained lately.

I needed to put everything on the table, including my schizophrenia. If Klayton still wanted to deal with me after that, then we could figure things out and go from there. I got up from the balcony and went back in the room with a purpose. I got out a purple Versace dress that fit my curves perfectly that I had packed specifically for this trip. I knew Klayton would snatch my ass up once he saw me walking around the casino in it. I grabbed a pair of purple edible panties and a purple lace push up bra that made my cleavage even bigger than it already was. If this didn't get his attention, nothing would. I was ready to rock Klayton's world.

I jumped in the shower and started bumping Usher on Apple Music, getting hype as fuck. If things went the way I wanted them to, this would be the first time I would willingly have sex and that was huge to me. Part of me was scared of it hurting like it did with Blach, but this was also something I wanted to experience for myself. There was no better man to experience my first time with than the man that

I am madly in love with, and I knew he would make sure I was taken care of.

A few minutes later, I got out of the shower and got dressed. I admired how the dress clung to every one of my curves and I knew I would be the center of attention. The thing was, I only wanted the attention of one man, and I was going to get it. I applied my MAC makeup and did my hair. It was flowing down my back. I finished getting ready and then headed down to the casino area to look for Klayton.

The smell of cigarettes invaded my nose as I walked into the casino area. I wrinkled my nose in disgust and kept walking. The sound of slot machines going off was in the background and then I got cold feet. *What if he found some strippers with a better body to entertain him? What if he had left the casino?* Those were my thoughts. I was about to turn back around and head back to the room when I felt him grab my shoulder.

"I thought you were in the room relaxing, Treasure. You better not have gotten dressed up for another nigga in this bitch. Otherwise, you are about to have his blood on your hands," Klayton whispered in my ears, and I was immediately turned on by his presence.

"I-I came to look for you, Klayton. I got cold feet and was about to head back to the room because I had no idea where you were at. This casino is huge," I admitted.

Klayton gazed at me lovingly and it felt like I was going to melt in his arms. "I want nothing more than for us to try and work through this storm together, Treasure. Are you sure you are in this for the long haul?"

Part of me felt insulted that he would ask me that because he knew that I basically sacrificed my relationship with my brother for him, but I also understood that Klayton has a hard time trusting women, and he was basically trusting me with his heart. At that moment, I forgot all about the club incident and other obstacles that were blocking our path towards being together. The only thing that mattered was Klayton and the love that we shared.

"I'm all in as long as you will have me, Klayton. I want you to make love to me, bae." I pressed my body against his, not caring who was watching us.

If I could shout from the rooftop how much I love Klayton Jackson, I would. We had issues that we needed to work thru, but I knew that we would be able to get through them together. I still needed to tell him about my schizophrenia, but that was a conversation I would definitely be having with him soon. Part of me was scared of how Klayton would react. Would he reject me and feel like I came with too much baggage?

"Are you sure you're ready, Treasure? I would never force you to do anything that you don't want to do. I don't want you to feel pressured into giving me pussy because I fucked up," Klayton explained. I could tell he was trying to be noble, but that wasn't what I wanted or needed at that moment.

"Klayton, if you aren't attracted to me, you can just say that." I was trying to hold back from crying, but I felt rejected by the man that I love.

Klayton lifted my head to meet his, and I could see the love that he had for me in his eyes. "Treasure, don't ever say such bullshit ever again. I was attracted to you from the second that I met you, and I still am. I just want to be sure you are truly ready. I wanted the moment that we made love for the first time to be special for you."

Klayton is ruthless and a savage in the streets, but he was definitely showing a soft side whenever he was with me. Love had a way of changing you and molding you. I was honored that I had the capability to make Klayton change, even if it was only a little bit. No one would ever be able to convince me that Klayton doesn't love me because I have witnessed his love for me in many different ways. He is my best friend, protector and soon to be my lover.

"We have been through so much together. It would only be fitting that I give you my special treasure between my legs. I want to know what it is like to make love to a man that I am in love with and experience sex. There is no one that I would choose to experience it with than you."

A few minutes later, Klayton was carrying me back in the room and placed me gently on the bed. "Lay down and don't move, Treasure. It's my turn to take care of you."

Good God, what did I ever do to deserve this man? I thought and did as I was told. Klayton came back with a bottle of champagne and a plate full of chocolate covered strawberries. I was touched and then remembered I was on medication. I haven't been taking my medication lately, so I figured having champagne wouldn't hurt. Hell, I recently had vodka with my mom, but this was a harsh reminder of my diagnosis and the fact that I probably needed to get back on my medication. Technically, I'm not supposed to drink alcohol while I am taking Zyprexa. I knew if I told Klayton that I couldn't drink, he would want to know why, and I wasn't ready to tell him just yet. Klayton passed me a glass of champagne then laid on the bed next to me with the plate of strawberries.

"How did you do all of this without me knowing?"

"When we were talking downstairs, I placed an order with room service, and it was ready when we got here. Treasure, you are the most beautiful woman I have ever seen, and I'm lucky to have you. I will die for you, Danielle or Genesis with no questions asked. Open your mouth," Klayton ordered.

I did exactly as I was told, and he placed one of the strawberries in my mouth. I took a bite and they tasted heavenly. Some of the juice from the strawberry was on my lips. The next thing I knew, Klayton was licking the juice off of my lips, and I was ready to get busy. What amazed me is the lengths that Klayton would go to just to make sure I was good even when I didn't deserve it.

The next thing that I knew, Klayton and I were making out, and my body felt like it was on fire. My love box was gushing like a river, and I just wanted to feel Klayton inside of me. Our tongues started dancing, and I could feel Klayton's hands remove my dress and them my purple lace bra. Klayton broke the kiss and just stared at my body for a moment. I almost felt self-conscious.

"You are perfect, Treasure. You were made just for me."

Klayton unhooked my bra and took my ample breasts in his hands. He started rubbing on them, then sucking on one of them. I let out a gentle moan. His tongue felt so good on my skin, I was kicking myself for waiting this long to give him my body. Klayton already had my heart but now he was about to have my body. Klayton started working his way down my body and kissing all the way down.

"Tell me if you get uncomfortable and want me to stop, bae. I will never do anything that you don't want me to do," Klayton reassured me. I understood why he was taking such precautions. I wanted him to know that I was ready for all of his good loving though.

"Klayton, if you don't make love to me, I swear I'm gonna think your ass is gay," I joked to lighten the mood, and he frowned.

"Don't ever speak such fuckery again, Treasure. I lick clits, not dicks!" Klayton frowned and then went back to work. He spread my legs open and started kissing me in between my thighs. He ripped my edible panties off with his teeth and threw them to the side. I gasped as he quickly went to work and started french kissing my clit. It felt so damn good, my body started shaking.

"Klayton!" I moaned as he continued feasting on my clit.

I lost track of time as I had numerous orgasms just from Klayton giving me head, and I haven't even had the main course yet, which was his dick. He finished going down on me and looked up at me. I couldn't help but feel slightly jealous, thinking how many other women did he give super head to?

"Lay there, Treasure. I don't want you putting in any work on your first time. After that, I will teach you how to ride a nigga's dick, but for now, let me do all of the work."

Part of me panicked because of my inexperience. What if I had a hard time learning how to ride? Klayton didn't leave me much time to worry too much because the next thing I knew, he was naked, and I was staring at all ten inches of his big, thick ass rod. I wondered how my little ass was going to take all of that dick, but I was up for the challenge.

"Klayton, I—"

"I promise I will be gentle with you, bae. Are you sure that you are ready for this?"

And now the moment of truth had arrived.

17

KLAYTON

I wanted to make love to Treasure more than anything I ever wanted in my life, but I wanted to be careful knowing Treasure's trauma history. Once I was inside of her, there was no turning back. I wanted to really be sure that she was ready for this. I was glad my phone was off because Sparkle had been texting me to see what this dick do, and there was no way I was going to take things there with her and risk losing Treasure for good. Besides, it doesn't make sense to shit where you eat, and it is inappropriate to go there with her since she is assigned to Danielle's case. I knew from jump Sparkle wanted the dick, and I made sure I did nothing to entertain her after our last conversation.

"Yes, Klayton, I'm ready for you. Be patient with me because I know I am not the most experienced but—"

"Don't worry about that. I know that you are more than enough to please me. I'm not going to put my entire dick inside of you yet because I don't want to hurt you. Once you adjust to my size, I will insert more until you can take all of me."

I wanted this to be just as pleasurable for Treasure as it would be for me. Hell, just giving her head was pleasing to me. Her cum tastes like sweet cotton candy, and I couldn't get enough of her. I knew that

Treasure was worried because of her lack of experience but honestly, I looked at that as a good thing. I could teach and mold her on how to please me, and I knew for a fact she wasn't out there letting every nigga sample her goodies. Hell, Treasure was the first pussy I put my mouth on in years because I don't give hoes head.

"I trust you, Klayton. Do what you feel is best."

Treasure gave me googly eyes, and I felt electric shocks throughout my body. No one could convince me that this woman was not meant for me. Treasure makes me soft and I hated that at times because love made me vulnerable. I should have been focused on finding Kamar, but I have been more worried about making sure Treasure and my daughter are both good. I grabbed a Magnum condom and put it on before sticking the tip of my tool inside of her wet, juicy love box. I could only imagine how it would feel to be inside of her raw, but I knew now was not the time to go half on a baby. I couldn't wait for the day that we started a family together but first, I had to get her to get custody of her daughter and get used to being a step-mother to Danielle. I also didn't want to get her pregnant while Kamar was out there on the loose because that would make Treasure even more of a target.

"Ouch! It hurts, Klayton," Treasure whined.

"Do you want me to stop, bae? The pain will go away, I promise you. It is your first time, so it does hurt, which is why I won't put all of me inside of you." I caressed her face.

If she wasn't with it, I would pull out right now because her comfort was my concern. Sex would always be there, but we were in the process of building a foundation together, and I wasn't going to risk that for momentary pleasure. I wanted Treasure to enjoy our lovemaking as much as I did, and I'm sensitive to making sure she is enjoying it. I have never had to take pussy from any woman and never will.

"No, keep going, Klayton. I want you to make me become a woman," Treasure whispered.

I could see the passion in her eyes and that made me keep going. I kept stroking her, slowly taking my time. Soon, I could feel her body start to adjust, so I inserted more of my dick inside of her until all of my dick was inside of her. I was surprised she ended up being able to take all of me inside of her, and I started giving her those loving slow strokes, making love to her body.

Treasure's body started shaking and her eyes started rolling to the back of her head. I could tell she was cumming. "Oh my God, Klayton!" Treasure screamed in pleasure.

It wasn't long before I was right behind her and busted inside of the condom before I pulled out of her. Treasure was easily the best I have ever had in the sack, and I have fucked plenty of hoes over the years. Granted, Treasure isn't experienced, but I loved that innocence about her, and I could teach her the things that I liked sexually. Treasure is pure and untainted in my eyes, and I will protect her with my life. She might have some young minded ways, but she's been through more than the average twenty-one-year-old, and I admire her strength. She wasn't looking at me as a come up, but her feelings for me were about me, not the money and the power that came with the lifestyle that I live.

"Treasure, I love you more than life itself. This is mine and a nigga better not come close to sniffing it." I cupped her pussy in my hand and Treasure giggled.

"Klayton, you are fucking crazy. I am not thinking about no other nigga and—"

"It better stay that way. Otherwise, I will go on a murder spree and my body count will go up in this bitch."

It felt good to see Treasure smile. Granted, we were still working thru a lot of our problems, but I was confident that we would get through them together. As mad as I have been at Treasure lately, I couldn't let her fend for herself against Luca at Jonah's funeral. It also wasn't the time or the place to set Luca straight, but I definitely would as soon as he has recovered from the surgery he had.

"You better check all of those hoes that were calling you on the plane. Now that I had a taste of that lethal weapon you're packing, it will be lights out for all of those bitches that think they can sample my goods. I will do a life bid behind that dick. Try me if you want to,

Klayton," Treasure called herself bossing up on me and it was funny. I swear my level of crazy was starting to rub off on her. She doesn't have to worry about other women because I only have eyes for her. I got all of my whorish ways out of my system years ago. Now I was ready to be a family man.

"There is no one out there that compares to you, Treasure. You are the woman that I want," I stated truthfully and held her in my arms. She always smells good and maintains her hygiene, unlike some of these hoes in the streets.

"Klayton, I want to tell you something, but please don't be mad, bae." Treasure stared at me and she looked scared. I didn't know what she could tell me that would have me upset with her, I was confused. I always wanted her to be able to feel like she could talk to me about anything. The fact that she was scared had me upset.

"Why would I be mad at you, Treasure? The only way I'm going to be mad at you is if you are lying to me about something," I stated calmly.

"I didn't lie to you, but you need to fully understand what you are getting into with me if you want me long term. When I was raped by Blach, I was diagnosed with schizophrenia, and I still take Zyprexa. I had stopped taking it, and I promise I will get back on my medication.. The incident at Jonah's funeral triggered an episode. I used to hear voices in my head, but I haven't had that happen in over a year. Please don't look at me like I'm crazy, Klayton," Treasure begged.

I was floored at what she just said, but it didn't make me look at her any differently. "Treasure, you aren't crazy. You are still the same woman that I love. Your past is the past, and I accept you for who you are. I will get on you about taking your medication, but I'm also going to do my own research about schizophrenia. I love you and I'm not leaving you because of it," I reassured Treasure.

When I said I was in it through the trenches for Treasure, I meant that. I would go to war for her. I understood why she was scared because mental health is still taboo in the black community and it is swept under the rug. If you ask me, it takes a strong person to admit that they need help and with everything that Treasure has gone through, I was completely surprised by the diagnosis. Her behavior patterns also fit because sometimes she is very hot and cold with her emotions and her behaviors. Now that I knew what was going on, I would do whatever I had to do to help her.

"Klayton, you amaze me. I just didn't want you to view me differently because of my diagnosis. I knew that you wouldn't, but it is hard because there is a stigma against mental illness. Hell, I know that it doesn't define who I am as a person, but society doesn't view it that way. I still see my counselor, and I think I need to start seeing her again more regularly. I have more things to work on," Treasure admitted.

None of us are perfect and I definitely am not perfect, so what would it look like if I judged Treasure over something that she couldn't control? I love her even more because it takes a strong person to admit that they need help. I vowed to be there every step of the way regardless if we worked out or not. I was going to be one of her biggest supporters, and I wanted Treasure to know that.

"I am proud of you admitting that to me because I know that wasn't easy. Hell, I'm not the easiest nigga to say shit to, so it had to have been hard for you to tell me that. Just know that we will conquer this together, and I have an idea. Actions speak louder than words and I want to prove to you that I am here for the long haul."

"What is your idea, Klayton?" Treasure looked at me curiously. I always knew that I wanted to settle down with her one day, but I really felt in my spirit that this was the right thing to do. Granted it was very impulsive considering all of the issues we have been having, and maybe it wasn't the smartest thing to do. However, life was too short to not be happy and take chances. I knew Treasure was the one for me.

"Marry me, Treasure. If you love a real nigga, marry my ass. We can get a marriage license in Clark County and go back to LA as husband and wife. What do you say?"

I had butterflies in the pit of my stomach as I awaited her answer. I hated the feeling of rejection, and I prayed Treasure accepted. I knew it was a hood ass marriage proposal, especially since I had no ring, but it felt more romantic to do it this way. Besides, what would it look like if a big ass nigga like myself got on one knee trying to flex? The only regret I would have is, she wouldn't have her dream wedding right off of the bat, but we could always plan a fancy ceremony once things settle down with Kamar.

Treasure had tears in her eyes, and she looked shocked. "Aww, bae, that proposal is sweet, specifically because this is coming from you."

"What do you say to a real nigga? Hell yea or hell naw?" I felt like I was going to be sick. Sure she said it was sweet, but what if she was going to say no? If she said no, my ego would definitely be bruised, and I wasn't sure that we would be able to come back from that. Maybe she was hesitant because of the fact that Luca wouldn't approve of us getting married, and I didn't want her to feel like she had to choose between me and her brother.

"Yes, I will marry you."

18

BRII

I finally adjusted to being admitted to Sunny dale and while I didn't want to be here, I knew that I needed to get better, not just for myself, but for the kids. I had been having nightmares ever since I learned about Jonah's death, and I had been blaming myself. I met Adrian during one of my group sessions, and he has been a source of comfort for me. Many times, when I would wake up screaming after a nightmare, I would find Adrian in my room holding and consoling me. We were starting to build a bond. I felt butterflies in my stomach and a connection to Adrian, but I knew it was way too soon for me to feel that way about someone since Jonah had just died.

"Brii, I got a plate for you already." Adrian tapped me on the shoulder, and I looked up at him. I didn't even know he was standing in front of me because I was lost in my own little world.

"Thanks, Adrian. I just got lost in thought for a second," I admitted. Since I had been here, I haven't been allowed any visitors. That didn't worry me too much because I didn't think anyone would really visit me. Sure, the kids love me, but how could I look at Leslie knowing that I am the reason that Jonah is dead?

"What is going on, Brii?" Adrian looked concerned. I was scared of how he could read me like a book because I hadn't known him very long.

Adrian is a very sexy man and had been making my lady parts quiver whenever I really look at him. Adrian is 5'10, shorter than what I normally like, with short brown hair and almond-shaped eyes. He looks like he is mixed with caramel colored skin. It threw me because I'm normally attracted to dark-skinned men like Jonah. Regardless of that, I needed to remember that it was too soon to even entertain the thought of being with someone new. I had too much baggage. I needed to get my life together first before I even thought about it.

"I really don't want to talk about it. Thank you for making me a plate in the cafeteria area, but I really am not hungry."

I ran back to my room, shut the door behind me and started sobbing. Not only did Jonah lose his life because of the poor choices that I made, but I knew my relationship with Nikki and the crew would never be the same. I wasn't even allowed to leave the hospital to go to Jonah's funeral. I wasn't sure that I would have been welcomed anyway. I haven't heard shit from Luca or anyone in the crew, and I knew I was now the black sheep that would take the blame for how everything played out.

A couple of minutes later, I felt Adrian hug me from behind, and he didn't say a word. He just held me as I continued to cry. Part of me wished that my suicide attempt was successful, so I wouldn't have to deal with all of the drama that I had created. I finally stopped crying and looked up at Adrian.

"I'm sorry. Your food is cold, and I'm over here acting like an emotional mess."

"Girl, that food is probably gone with all of the vultures that wanted seconds. Don't worry about it. Something tells me that you needed a friend, and I'm here for you. I won't judge you because we are all in here dealing with our own issues," Adrian reassured me.

I was curious as to why Adrian was here. He looked too well put together to be hospitalized with me. I didn't know much about Adrian because he never volunteered much information about himself during group, but he would always give words of encouragement to everyone else. What was his story and why was he here?

"Tell me more about you, Adrian. I'm about to spill my guts about me, but I know almost nothing about you. You look too sane to be here with the rest of us."

The girl in the room next door to me is a cutter and has schizophrenia. Sometimes, late at night, she bangs her head on walls, and she hears voices in her head. Adrian looked too normal to be here with the rest of us.

"I don't tell people much about me because I don't trust easily. Anything I tell you must stay between me and you. I don't even trust the people in Sunnydale. See, they want to pick, probe and psychoanalyze you because they want to fix you. Sometimes people are just broken from situations that are out of their control." Adrian looked at me.

"I promise. Trust me, I'm going to share some very personal stuff with you, so I guess you will have something over me as well."

I was unsure whether I should confide in Adrian, but it felt good to have someone who wasn't a counselor trying to probe and fix me. I needed someone to just be a friend. It appeared Adrian fit the bill, but I needed to know something about him first. There was something mysterious that drew me to him, and I was fighting this pull. I knew Jonah was rolling over in his grave right now at the thought of me moving on so quickly. And the fact remains, I know very little about Adrian.

"My name is Adrian Jones, and I am thirty years old. I am in here because I have an eating disorder. I know it sounds crazy because you think men don't have eating disorders, but I suffer from bulemia. When I was a kid, I was a chubby kid, and my mom always had me on all of these fad diets. At first, she thought I would outgrow it and then I continued gaining weight. She would call me a fat ass and ugly motherfucker on a daily basis, and it made me determined to lose the weight. I hated my body, I hated my average looks, and I was bullied in school as well. I heard of some girls trying to lose weight by binging and purging, and I figured I would only do that for a month or so until I lost the weight I wanted to lose. Once I started and saw the pounds coming off, I became more confident and started growing into my looks, but I got addicted to binging and purging. When I turned twenty years old, I had gotten down to one hundred pounds and was hospitalized. I got the help I needed to stop at that time." Adrian paused.

"You look perfectly healthy to me, Adrian. If you stopped ten years ago then why are you here?" I asked, confused.

"I relapsed and started binging and purging again over a year ago after a bad break up. I was engaged to get married. My fiance left me and got pregnant by my ex-best friend. I caught them in bed together, and it sent me down a path of destruction. My parents begged me to check myself into Sunnydale because I lost over forty pounds and probably would have ended up dying if I continued going down that path of destruction."

Adrian held me, and I was touched by his story. There is a common misconception that men don't suffer from eating disorders and that they are weak for showing emotion. If anything, I admired how brave Adrian was to share his story with me because he didn't know me from a can of paint. Now I understood why he really didn't open up much during group sessions, and I hoped I could encourage him to do so, so he could receive the help that he needed.

"Thank you so much for sharing that with me, Adrian. It took a lot for you to share and I appreciate that. I know there are battles that you face as a man that I will never fully understand, but I hope I can be there for you the way you have been for me." I needed to stop crying and put my big girl panties on because there were many people that go through situations worse than mine. Granted, my situation is difficult to deal with and it would take time to repair all of the relationships that are broken, but I was determined to do so. I had listened to different people's stories in group, and they all touched me, but none to the level that Adrian's story did.

"I just appreciate you not judging me for my struggle. Society tells me as a man I should be taller, sexier, the breadwinner of the house and breed masculinity. For years, I tried to act like an alpha male when that really isn't my personality, and I lost myself. I'm learning now that I have to love myself before I can find another woman that will love me. Now that I shared a bit of myself, what is your story, Brii? I know that you have nightmares and have gone through a lot, but you never go into detail too much," Adrian pressed me for details.

"I made some very bad decisions that changed the course of my life. It's crazy because I had gotten my happily ever after with the love of my life, Jonah, and I managed to fuck it up." I started crying again. If I didn't go out that fateful night, I wouldn't have made myself a target for Kamar and maybe Jonah and I would be working on improving our marriage. Now it was too late, and I had no one to blame but myself.

"What happened? It could be that you are too hard on yourself because you love hard. Sometimes it is hard for us to see how our actions affect others at the time," Adrian whispered as he continued holding me. I felt safe in his arms, and it gave me the encouragement I needed to continue telling my story.

"Jonah is an amazing man and that is the true love of my life. I don't even deserve to experience love ever again since he is dead. Jonah and I met when my twin sister, AJ, and I were in the streets trying to find our siblings who had been kidnapped and held hostage. He helped me find them and was willing to raise them as his own kids. We got married and that should have been our happily ever after. The thing is, with the childhood that I experienced having to look after my siblings while our mother was out there being a fucking crackhead, I didn't want to have any more kids. Jonah and I had my siblings and a child from his ex that we were raising together; that should have been enough. Granted, Leslie turned out to not be Jonah's child, but we had developed a bond with him, so we took him in. Where I messed up was, I assumed that Jonah would be ok with not having any biological kids—"

"You guys never had that conversation before you got married though? That is a major life decision that could be a deal breaker for you. Was money an issue for you guys?" Adrian interrupted.

"Money was never an issue because Jonah was that nigga to see in the streets. He was known as Cane, but he had retired from the streets before we got married. Jonah always made sure we were good financially, and I had been planning to start a business. Jonah really wanted a biological child of his own, and I have no desire to ever give birth to anyone's kids. I know it sounds selfish but between raising my siblings and Leslie being so young, I figured that would be fine. Then I could spend time traveling and taking time to really live my life. The problem was, that was the bottom of the barrel with our marital problems. One night, Jonah and I had one of our worst fights about having children, and I went out to the bar to have a drink. I ended up blacking out and in this nigga's bed the next day, so he had date raped me. I should have told Jonah that I was raped, but I was embarrassed and blamed myself for what happened. What made the entire situation worse was I found out I was pregnant, and Jonah caught me at the abortion clinic. It made everything worse because I lied and told him that I cheated on him," I admitted, and Adrian's mouth dropped open.

"I assume you didn't tell Jonah because he would have gone and killed the fuck ass nigga that violated you. I know if you were my wife, I would have gone on a murder spree, and I'm not about that life."

"That was part of it. I knew that Jonah would have killed Kamar and I didn't want that to happen, so I lied. I guess you can say I protected my rapist and it sickens me to say that. I didn't want his ass going to prison when I should have sat my ass at home that night. I was arguing with some friends on whether to tell Jonah the truth when he overheard our argument and it created even more tension in our relationship. I was hurt because I was selfish and thought he still should have been there for me, so one night, I decided to commit suicide. I swallowed a bottle of pills, and Jonah found my body." I stopped for a second and I could feel myself getting choked up.

"Take your time, Brii. We can change the subject if this is getting too uncomfortable for you." Adrian continued holding me, stroking his hand through my hair; it was relaxing.

"Jonah was devastated, and that man loved the shit out of me,

Adrian. What burns me up the most is I didn't appreciate what I had in my husband. He ended up shooting himself in the head in front of my friends, and he died blaming himself for my actions. I was the worst wife and that is why I am here. I don't understand why I'm alive and Jonah is dead. Why?" I sobbed. Adrian continued holding me and didn't say a word as I continued crying. I kept crying until I ended up falling asleep.

19

KAMAR

A nigga was feeling frustrated because none of the shit I was doing to bring Klayton down was working so far. I had some more of Klayton's traps hit but because he is also the fucking connect, he really wasn't taking too much of a loss. Then the Bethany situation made shit hot, so I ended up laying low in Mexico because no one would think to look for my ass in Tijuana. I found this sexy little broad named Brianna who I dragged along for the ride, and I was determined to get some fucking pussy. I might have bitten off more than I could chew, and it pissed me off because I wanted to be in Klayton's position, especially with that fine ass bitch Treasure. I decided to call up some of my niggas from Philly and have them come down here to help me. I decided to call my nigga Pablo and have him bring Diego and assemble a crew to come to assist me in my mission. I was a bit overwhelmed, and Pablo was the only one that knew that I was coming out here. He tried to tell me that I was on a suicide mission, but all I saw was more money signs by expanding to the West Coast.

I grabbed my phone and called Pablo Ramirez. He always was a straight shooter, so I knew he would give good advice. Pablo was not only one of my right-hand men, but someone I would trust with my life. When the shit hit the fan, I just knew that he was going to come and help me get out of this situation.

"Yo', what's up, nigga?" Pablo knew it was me because I was calling from one of the many disposable burner phones I had bought in Walmart on the way to Tijuana. As soon as I finished this call, I was going to get rid of this phone, so Klayton and his people wouldn't be able to track me for long. I knew he was going to kick my ass for getting myself in this predicament, but I didn't know things were going to go left with the plan the way it did. I had assumed after the explosion, I would easily be able to take over for Klayton when that clearly has not been the case.

"Man, I got myself in some shit. I need you to get Diego and a crew assembled and meet me in Tijuana," I ordered.

"What the fuck did you get yourself into? I told you that you shouldn't have gone down there starting shit especially by yourself. I'm honestly surprised your ass is still alive, nigga," Pablo lectured me. I deserved it, but I didn't want to hear anything that he was saying. Besides, I couldn't go back and change what happened, so Pablo would have to get over it and come help me get out of this jam.

"Man, Klayton is a little preoccupied from the stunts that I'm pulling. Granted I managed to hit some shit, but it isn't making a fucking dent because he's the damn plug. Any losses he's taking, he can easily replace, so it isn't as easy to force his ass out like I thought it was," I complained. I wish I would have thought things through a bit more and come up with a better plan, but I thought since Klayton had a reputation for being a womanizer and reckless, it would be easy to get his ass caught up.

"Kamar, you didn't even need to do this because we were eating straight. Greed is going to be your downfall. Now you put your life at risk and ours too if we come down there," Pablo complained.

"If you come down here? Don't forget that I'm the motherfucking boss," I threatened. Pablo must have gotten a little big headed since I left him in charge of running shit. I needed to remind him who was the fucking boss.

"Nigga, I will get a team to come down to help you, but I don't want any parts of this bullshit you are trying to drag me into. Let's keep it real, you went down there to take over for Klayton, but you had no plans on spreading the wealth anyway. There is no way I'm putting my life on the line and getting nothing out of it. I suggest you lay low for a good while and then come back to Philly where you belong and where we're fucking eating if you want to ever enjoy the fruits of our labor. Hell, I don't even know what kind of bullshit you were down there doing." I should have dragged Pablo and some of the crew down with me in the first place. Maybe I would have gotten more accomplished than I did. Greed was my downfall because I didn't want to pay any of the men to come help me with this mission.

"Man, I blew up part of Klayton's house and almost killed his little bitch. I have been knocking on his property and shit too, and I raped a hoe while I was out here. She had some of the best pussy I ever tasted, especially for a fat bitch and—" I felt no need to lie to Pablo because he knows how I get down with women. Back in Philly, I had a reputation for drugging women because I didn't believe in hearing the word no. If I wanted pussy, I was going to get it willingly, or I was going to take the fucking pussy. As far as I was concerned, if the women would just give me what I wanted in the first place, I wouldn't have to resort to desperate measures.

"On second thought, I'm not sending anyone out there for the fuck shit you have been doing, Mar. You have been doing all sorts of crazy shit then you live with the fucking consequences, nigga. I know if you had done that shit to me or people I know, your ass would be dead and gone. We all know Klayton Jackson's name rings bells all along the West Coast. Remember that you can run, but he will find you at some point, nigga. You are on your own."

Pablo hung up on my ass and I was seeing red. How dare this nigga hang up on me like he was running shit? I made a vow to make Pablo pay for his actions once I made it back to Philly, but for now, I had other issues to worry about. I started pacing back and forth in the little cheap dump I had paid up for overnight. I didn't want to stay in one place for too long knowing Klayton was going to be after my head. I also figured they wouldn't look in the roach hotels and it would help me conserve funds. Pablo was supposed to be on my side dammit, and he should be running to help me get out of this situation I put myself in. I put that nigga in the position that he was in now. Although, to be honest, he always put in more work than I did. He did a lot of the dirty work with my operations in Philly and New York, so I knew he wasn't riding my coattails and most of my success is due to him. However, without me, Pablo wouldn't be where he is today.

"Excuse me, Kamar? I was hoping I could make you feel a little better. You look stressed out."

Brianna batted her eyes at me, and her fake breasts were falling out of her blouse. I picked this desperate little bird up from the gas station, so I prayed she didn't have any shit that I couldn't get rid of. I should have been thinking on how I was going to get out of this fucking mess I was in, but I could feel my dick poking through my pants like a fucking jack-in-the-box.

"Get on your knees and let me see what your mouf do," I ordered, and she quickly got to work.

I love submissive bitches. Hopefully, she knew how to give a nigga head. Otherwise, I was going to have to punish her ass.

She freed my rod from my boxers and quickly went to work with a pathetic attempt on giving me head. She took the mushroom tip in her mouth and started sucking on it. At first, it felt good until I felt her bite my dick, and I was about to beat her ass.

I pulled my dick out of her mouth and yelled, "What the fuck, you stupid bitch? You bit my damn dick! Did someone ever teach you how to give head?"

I was hunched over on the ground in pain but finally managed to get back up. I punched her in the face, and her face whipped backward. She hit her head on the wall and fell to the ground crying.

"I-I'm sorry! I didn't mean to bite your dick—"

"Bitch, shut the fuck up!" I spit in her face. I was about to take all of my frustrations out on her. Brianna was about to be my human punching bag whether she liked it or not. I yanked her by her head and threw her ass on the bed.

"Please stop! It was an accident and—"

I punched her in the face to get her ass to shut up. The very least I could do was sample the pussy and see if it was any damn good. Her ass was knocked out, so I guess I was going to have to bust a Trump, grab her by the pussy then take the shit. I quickly inserted my tool inside of her did a few quick grunts and unloaded my seed inside of her. I didn't give a fuck about using a condom because the bitch wouldn't live much longer anyway. I finished, pulled out, put my dick back in my boxers and realized that I wasn't done punishing her just yet. I grabbed the lamp that was on the nightstand next to me and smashed it on her head. Blood spilled everywhere. I knew if Brianna wasn't dead then, she was very close to it. In the background, I could hear someone playing fiesta music in the background, but I still didn't want to use a gun to kill her. I wanted to torture her and end her miserable existence. I grabbed a pocket knife out of my pocket and sliced her fake breasts off one by one, watching the blood change the color on the sheets and pillowcases she was lying on. I'm one sick motherfucker and I don't make any apologies for it.

My dick got hard at the thought of dismembering Klayton's body. I couldn't wait until the time comes for me to get the rewards that were waiting for me. Brianna was definitely dead by now, but I wasn't done torturing her. All of my frustrations about my plans failing and the fact that Brii disappeared off of the face of the earth had me frustrated. I had been trying to find her recently to collect on what was due, and that was another sample of her good pussy. Just the thought had me aroused, and I couldn't help myself, so I decided to fuck Brianna's dead corpse.

I let out some pumps and came quicker than I did the first time I fucked her. Then I realized I still had that burner phone on me, and that shit could have been tracked, especially since that conversation with Pablo didn't end the way I would have liked. I needed to get the fuck out of dodge, and I couldn't stay here where there was a dead body. I decided to leave the phone here and get my ass back on the run until I figured out what my next move was going to be.

20

LUCA

I was counting my lucky stars that I didn't die when I got shot at Jonah's funeral, and this was a second chance at life. I was being discharged from the hospital, and my mom was planning to stay with me to help take care of me until I got back on my feet. Right after the shooting, the doctors had to do emergency surgery to remove the bullet that was in my stomach and stop the blood loss. Now I was recovering, but the doctors had to stitch me back up. I was ordered to rest for the next couple of weeks, but my ass was ready to find out who the hell was behind that shooting. I bet it was the nigga that was coming for Klayton, but I don't even have the energy to try to address him right now. My mind was all over the place at the moment because I was grieving Jonah's death, and my relationship with my sister was the worst it has ever been in a while.

"How are you feeling, Luca?" My mom asked, squeezing my hand.

My father and Genesis had left to go get something to eat from the cafeteria. It was good to have some private time with my mother. My biggest regret was how I disrespected my sister and my niece at the funeral, and I owed them a huge apology. My feelings were hurt because I felt like my sister should have been there for me, but she was off with that fuck nigga Klayton. I had to admit that I basically pushed her into his arms, and I hated it. I wanted to fix my relationship with Treasure, and I needed to figure out how to do that because I just had a wake-up call. Life was too short to hold on to petty grudges, but could I ever really accept Klayton being with my sister?

As the older brother, I always thought no nigga was good enough for Treasure and when Klayton ended up getting his dick sucked by Gigi, that proved that I was right about him all along. Granted, he couldn't have known about the connection with me and Gigi. And we weren't together at that time, but I was still in my feelings about it. I knew that I had no room to make demands because I have been acting like a fuck boy, but I felt betrayed by Treasure. It didn't make sense to me how she could pick Klayton over me.

"I'm feeling better. Have you talked to Treasure?" I asked. Part of me wanted to call Treasure and check on her, but I also knew that she wasn't fucking with me on any level, and rightfully so. The things that I said to her was fucked up. I knew that I had no right to be hurt that I haven't seen her since I had surgery since I wasn't there for her when she was in a coma, but I'm a selfish nigga. I miss when we were younger, and we were close. I used to hate when I would be forced to take her with me when I would go play with my friends but now, I would give anything to go back to those days.

"No, I haven't, but she is in good hands with Klayton."

"Why are you and dad ok with my sister being with a nigga that betrayed me? I don't understand why you guys are on her side!" I blurted out. I want my sister to be happy, but I didn't understand why she wanted to be with Klayton. I was convinced it was only because I declared him the forbidden fruit. I was used to being the man of the house and calling the shots. Now I felt like I was losing any control that I did have over my sister. I didn't like not being in control and it left a bitter taste in my mouth.

"You need to let the past go, son. What happened with AJ was three years ago and the person you needed to blame was AJ, not Klayton. She was the one that owed you loyalty at the time and betrayed your trust." My mom pointed her finger in my face. That was true, but

AJ was gone, and I needed someone to continue pointing the finger at. What the fuck it looked like if I continued blaming a ghost?

"Klayton never changed though. When shit got tough with Treasure being in a coma, he went out there and got his dick sucked by my damn girl. Granted, we weren't together at the time, but still, he has to have everything that I fucking have."

I was getting angry just thinking about it. Klayton violated the bro code. We weren't close friends, but he still violated in my eyes. I would never try to kee-kee with that nigga even if it would make Treasure happy. I just didn't see how I could learn to accept Klayton being a part of the family if Treasure really was serious about him. I didn't want her to date, but I was starting to realize that I couldn't stop her from living her life. I did think I had the right to approve who she should be with, but it is my job to be overprotective of her as her big brother.

"Luca, you just said you and Gigi weren't together at the time. And how was Klayton supposed to know that you were interested in her anyway? Was he supposed to call Miss Cleo for a psychic prediction? Listen son. I want you to live life and be happy, but you have to let go of the beef. Klayton made a mistake, but we all know that he wasn't behaving rationally when Treasure was in a coma. Hell, if you had been visiting your sister in the hospital, you would have seen him crying for Treasure every day. He is madly in love with her, and there isn't a better man out there for her, so you need to get over this bullshit, Luca. Klayton was there for her when you weren't, so who are you to judge him? I know damn well he wouldn't disrespect her the way that you did at Jonah's funeral. In fact, you don't even need to worry about Treasure right now."

"I'm always going to worry about my baby sister and my niece, especially if she continues to deal with Klayton. I can't believe that nigga is fooling all of you because he is still the same reckless nigga with community dick. And what the fuck makes Treasure so damn special? He might be enamored with her right now, but I guarantee you he will cheat on her again. I will be right here to tell all of you 'I told you so' when he proves me right again. Fuck the beef that I have with Klayton, I never wanted her to end up with a street nigga. You know Treasure and Genesis will be the first thing that niggas use as a fucking target just to get at Klayton's ass."

"Luca, that could have been the case as well when you and Jonah were living that damn life, so cut the bullshit, son. I love you more than you ever know, so I apologize if you feel like I'm not taking your side. You are deadass wrong to stop your sister from living her life. Everything you have tried to do to control her has failed and the only thing your actions are doing is pushing her further into Klayton's arms. Son, Treasure is this close to not having a relationship with you at all for the stunt you pulled at Jonah's funeral, and it hurts my heart to see you two at odds like this. I need you to fix this shit, Luca!" My mom's hands were trembling, and I could tell she was trying to stop herself from crying.

I had to control Treasure because she had no idea what she was doing. I was looking out for her because she was incapable of making her own decisions. I felt bad. I never wanted my mom to be sad, but why was it on me to fix this shit? If Treasure had left Klayton alone in the first place, none of this would have happened.

"Mom, I love you, but if Treasure wants to talk to me, she knows where I live and what my phone number is. I shouldn't have to reach out to her because she is having a temper tantrum." At some point, my sister would get over it, and we would work things out. She knows that I didn't mean what I said to her and that was in the heat of the moment, so I was willing to wait until she got over her little shit fit.

"Luca, I am so disappointed in you. You are one of the most selfish niggas I have seen in a long time. I would have thought the fact that you got shot and survived would have been a wake-up call for you, but you still only give a fuck about yourself and your feelings. You conveniently forget that you disrespected Treasure at Jonah's funeral and all she was trying to do was comfort you because she knew how much you loved Jonah. You are not the only person that ever goes through anything, Luca. I raised you to be a man, not a fuck boy." Mom pointed her finger in my face, and I bit it.

I was tired of taking shit from everyone, even if my parents were right. At this point in my life, I felt like no one understood me and the pain that I was living with on a daily basis with my brother, Jonah, dead and gone. My mom looked shocked and then she used her other hand to slap me in the face. Her little hands packed a powerful punch, and I felt remorseful for biting her finger.

"Your father is going to have to talk some sense into you or beat your ass. I just can't deal with you anymore. I will never give up on you because you are my son, but I don't have any words for you right now." My mom stepped back and started to leave the room.

"Mom, I'm sorry. Please come back!" Reality was finally starting to hit me. I was pushing everyone that gave a fuck about me away, and I was helpless to stop it.

My mom stopped right as she got in front of the door and stared at me for a minute before walking out of the door. Right afterward, I heard my dad walk in the room with someone else.

"Luca, what the hell did you do to hurt your mother? She ran out of here crying. I ran into someone that wanted to see you, but I just might have to put my foot up your damn ass."

"Dad, I fucked up. Mom was checking me about my recent behavior, and I bit her finger—"

I didn't even get to finish my statement before my dad punched me in the face. "I hope Klayton beats the shit out of you, and I won't stop his ass from doing it. You are trying to push everyone away. I will never give up on you son. You are not the only one that is hurting right now, and I need you to get it together. I know that you lost Jonah and you miss Gigi. You know what, Gigi, come here so I can stop myself from choking this nigga."

Those were the last words my dad said before he left the room. I was speechless at the sight of Gigi's curvaceous ass standing by my bedside.

21

GIGI

I was just about to leave the emergency room after finding out that Marina had died when I ran into Luca's father. I didn't see him, rather he saw me and chased me down before I got in the car and told me Luca had gotten shot at Jonah's funeral. My head was spinning because there was so much that had been going on. No wonder Luca hadn't reached out to me lately.

"Are you ok, Gigi? My son needs you, but you look like you are going through some things right now." Giovanni hugged me in a father-daughter type of hug, and I started crying. I couldn't believe Marina got caught up with a nigga that isn't shit and that ended up with her losing her life.

"My best friend just died. I had gotten an apartment and her ex had found her and showed up at my apartment before he shot her. My sister, Candice, ended up killing Anthony and the police are questioning her about what happened," I explained.

"I have some connections, Gigi, so don't worry about your sister. I'm so sorry to hear about your loss. We will be here for you during this tough time. I'm going to text the lawyer Klayton has us use and send her down to the police station that your sister is at," Giovanni explained.

"Candice is in the emergency room talking to the police. I just needed to come outside and get some fresh air for a minute. I hate hospitals, and my entire world is crashing down on me. What are you doing at the hospital?" I asked curiously. I prayed there was nothing wrong with Luca, but I had a feeling I was about to get more bad news.

Giovanni looked like he didn't want to tell me what was going on, but he finally responded. I know that you have a lot on your plate, and I don't want to burden you with anything else but you need to know that Luca got shot."

I turned my head and vomited on the ground. Luca and I might not be on good terms, but I had fallen in love with him regardless of how much I fought it. The possibility that Luca might be dead was more than I could handle at that moment. I had just lost my best friend and haven't even had time to really process that, then I find out Luca had gotten shot. I would have fallen to the ground if Giovanni hadn't caught me. I was grateful that he had my back.

"Please tell me he is ok. I can't handle another loss. I really can't." I broke down crying.

Giovanni held me, and I let it all out. I was embarrassed because I have never been the type of female to wear my emotions on my sleeve. I was the mother hen type that had to stay strong for everyone else. The fact that Giovanni saw me vulnerable was something I didn't like.

"Gigi, Luca is going to be ok. He is being discharged today, and he is mandated to go on bed rest for the next couple of weeks. He was shot in the stomach and surgery was done to dislodge the bullet that was stuck in his chest. He got to the hospital just in time because he could have bled out. I know you are going through a lot, but if you want to see him, I will take you to him."

I was conflicted. I really did want to see him, but I also needed to make sure my sister was good. "I do want to go check on him, but my sister is in the emergency room talking to the police, and I don't want to leave her for too long. They might try to pin murder charges on her, although if you ask me, that shit was self-defense.

He was waving that gun around like he was going to shoot all of us."

Giovanni showed me his phone. "The lawyer, Tiffani Stephenson, is on her way as we speak. We can wait for her and then I can take you to Luca's room if you like."

"Thank you, I appreciate that. How are you holding up? I can tell this drama is taking a toll on you." I wanted Giovanni to know that I was here for him as well. I know the entire family was going through it.

"I'm holding up as well as can be expected. I appreciate you asking. Hope is going to have to move back with Luca until he is able to take care of himself. It is a lot on the family. Treasure and Luca aren't on good terms because he feels like she chose Klayton over him, and he disrespected Treasure at the funeral. Just trying to get this family back together is going to be a lot of work, but I refuse to allow the drama to tear us apart. Gigi, Luca really needs to get help to get over the past and stop trying to control his sister. If anyone can get through to him, it's you. I know that I am asking a lot from you, but can you please try to talk to him?" Giovanni pleaded.

His eyes were bloodshot red like he had been crying and there was no way that I could say no to him. However, if the Klayton he mentioned was the same Klayton that I had given oral pleasures to at the club, I knew shit was going to get a whole lot worse before it got better.

An hour later, I was walking into Luca's room. Giovanni had kept his word and Tiffani showed up to take Candice down to the police station for questioning. She promised me that she would drop Candice off and keep me updated on what happened. I knew Tiffani was a pit bull in the legal field. Her name rings bells even more than Luca's, so I knew Candice was in good hands. I stood outside of Luca's room for a few minutes. I was nervous of how the conversation was going to go with him considering how he had been spazzing out on people. I prayed he didn't know that I had messed with Klayton. I didn't even know they were connected, and I was single at the time. I could hear Luca and Giovanni arguing and thought maybe I should come another time because I really didn't think Luca was in a good mood. However, I finally managed to get the courage to step into the room.

I stepped in and was shocked to see Luca staring at me emotionless. I knew at that moment that he somehow knew about what happened with Klayton, but I couldn't bring myself to move. It felt like my feet were stuck and time had stopped.

"What are you doing here, Gigi?" That was all Luca asked me, and I had tears in my eyes. I really did not need Luca's shit right now, but I also was not going to allow him to push me away.

"I just heard you were shot. I wanted to check on you and make sure you were ok," I stated calmly. I felt anything but calm at that moment, but I was going to try to not let Luca take me out of character.

"Why do you give a fuck, Gigi? You must think I'm boo boo the fucking fool. To think you had me fooled when you are really a gold-digging ass slut bucket." Luca disrespected me, and my temper was rising.

My hands were visibly shaking because I don't let niggas take me out of character, but Luca had the right one. "Nigga, your ego is bruised, but I'm going to let you have that. I was good before you. I don't need a man to financially support me. I have been working since I was a teenager, and I never had a need to rely on a nigga to support me. The only thing saving you from an ass beating is the fact that you got shot—"

"Did you fuck him, bitch?" Luca interrupted me. I had to hold tears back and try to stop myself from putting my hands on him because he had me fucked up.

"First of all, let's get something straight. My name is Gigi, not bitch. And if you are referring to what happened with Klayton, no, I didn't fuck him. I see that is what has your panties in a bunch right now. Yes, I sucked Klayton's dick, but I did that before we made things official, and I didn't even know that you two know each other at the time. What you are not going to do is disrespect me because of something that I did when I was single. You might have gotten away with that kind of shit in the past, but let me tell you, I am not the fucking one. I came to see if you were ok—"

"You still shouldn't have fucked with him on any level, Gigi! That shit makes me look like a fucking clown. Someone sent me a text of you sucking his dick in a club bathroom. You might have been single, but you were out there acting like a thot when you represented yourself to be something different with me. I wanted to fucking marry you one day, Gigi! You had my ass wide open in ways that I haven't been since AJ, and I looked like a fucking clown!" Luca yelled, and Giovanni ran back inside the room.

He stood by my side trying to make sure Luca and I weren't about to come to blows. Today was one of the worst days of my life and to end up dealing with Luca's bullshit had me overwhelmed to where I was ready to say fuck everything. I didn't have anything else to emotionally give to Luca. He clearly had his mind made up on the situation before he had even had a conversation with me about it.

"Luca, I'm in love with you. I tried fighting it every step of the way but regardless, I ended up falling for you. You already have your mind made up that I'm a whore, and that is ok. I won't beg for your forgiveness, and I certainly won't beg you to be with me. Just know that you are not the only one that is going through things right now. You are very selfish. You never once asked me how I was doing, especially with me handling things for you at the firm. I love you and I wish we could work through this, but I will not kiss your ass in the process. I'm praying for you to get better and get your life together, Luca. You really need help because you are a broken man, and you don't even see it." I turned to walk away but Giovanni grabbed my shoulder.

"Can you wait for me outside please, Gigi? I want to talk to you for a minute," he pleaded.

"Fine," I agreed reluctantly and went to walk outside. I heard Luca and Giovanni talking. I had nothing else to say to Luca right now. I was kind of relieved everything was put on the table, and I truly didn't know if Luca and I would ever make things work. I refused to feel guilty about things that I did before Luca and allow him to shame and embarrass me.

"Gigi, I'm sorry for how Luca disrespected you, and I will talk to him. Where are you going to go since that happened in your apartment?" Giovanni asked.

"I was just going to go get a hotel until I got another apartment. There is no way that I can stay in the apartment that my best friend was murdered in. Hell, I don't even want the things that are in that apartment other than the work stuff I have there," I explained.

"I insist you stay with Hope and Genesis at my new house. Luca is going to require some care and considering he pissed my wife off earlier, it might be best if I go stay with him for a couple of weeks and you can stay at my house with Hope, Genesis and Treasure. Your sister is more than welcome to come too." Giovanni walked me out of the hospital and back to my car.

"Luca can kiss my entire ass, sir, but if he needs me, I will still be there for him as a friend. I can't allow him to disrespect me. What happened with Klayton happened was before I was with Luca. I had no idea they knew each other, or I would have never gone there with him. I don't want to impose on you guys."

"You are coming to stay at my house and that is final. Hope already took the car home, so I will drive your car to my place," Giovanni ordered and held his hand out for my car keys. I reluctantly gave them to him and got in on the passenger side. I knew there was no point arguing with him over it. I had bigger issues to deal with.

"Do you know who sent Luca that text message because there was no way for Luca to know what happened." I was curious about how he found out.

Giovanni glanced over at me before he started the engine. "There is a nigga named Kamar that is coming for Klayton due to some street shit. He was the one that sent a screenshot to Luca and Treasure."

"Wait, Treasure is dating Klayton?" I asked and my face turned pale as a ghost. Not only was this shit getting messy as hell, but if this was the Kamar that I think it was, shit was really about to hit the fan.

"Klayton and Treasure are having relationship issues, but they are trying to work things out." Giovanni hit the breaks. I knew he figured out how we were all connected.

"Listen, I don't think it is a good idea that I stay at your house. This is a situation that is not going to end well."

22

KLAYTON

"Do you, Treasure Milan Glover, take Klayton Iman Jackson to be your lawfully wedded husband?" This fake Elvis looking motherfucker asked. If he didn't stop clocking a nigga's dick, I would end up shooting the fucker's dick off. Everyone knows that I have screws loose and I have no sense.

"Nigga, would you stop staring at my fiance's dick with your gay ass?" Treasure yelled and my dick got hard.

She was starting to act as crazy as I was. I knew that my dick was starting to make her crazy. That is what good dick does to the woman that you love. I have nothing against gay men, but I don't swing that way. I would rather not have to shoot a nigga down because my mouth has no chill at all.

"My apologies. May I continue?" The dude asked.

"Do you want to go to another wedding chapel and get this done, bae?" Treasure and I had gotten up at five am and went to get a marriage license in Clark County. We had no problems getting it done. This wasn't the most ideal way to get married, but all I cared about was making Treasure my wife. I had been learning that life was too short to not go after what makes you happy. I didn't want to waste another second without making Treasure my wife.

"Naw, let's get this done, bae." Treasure stared at me lovingly. I swear I never felt this way about a woman before. I never knew what love was until I met Treasure Glover, soon to be Jackson.

"Go ahead and hurry up," I gestured at the nigga and pointed to the gun I had on me. I always make sure I'm strapped and managed to buy a gun from some niggas when I got here since I couldn't carry one on the airplane.

He looked at Treasure and repeated his question. Treasure looked back at me. "I do."

"Do you, Klayton Iman Jackson, take Treasure Milan Glover to be your lawfully wedded wife?" Fake Elvis asked.

"Hell yeah a mothafuckin' nigga do!" I licked my lips and didn't even wait for him to announce that I could kiss the bride. I picked Treasure up and stuck my tongue her throat. We were in a full make-out session until Fake Elvis tapped me on the shoulder.

I ended the kiss, pulled my gun out and shot fake Elvis in the head three times. "Fuck you, motherfucker. Interrupting my first kiss with my lovely bride just cost you your damn life. Bae, let's go!"

I picked Treasure up and carried her bridal style to the limo I had hired for our big day. The wedding was a bit of a spectacle, even for me. I didn't count on catching a body on my own wedding day.

"I love you, Treasure and when everything settles down, I promise to give you the wedding of your dreams. You deserve better than getting married in front of fake Elvis, bae, and a nigga fucks with you tough."

"Klayton, that doesn't matter to me. I married you because I'm in love with you, and I want to spend the rest of my life with you. You better not think about fucking another woman or it will be slow singing and flower bringing," Treasure warned, and my dick got hard as fuck. Treasure was becoming as crazy as I was.

"Shitttt, same goes for you. Any nigga you think about fucking, his blood on your hands, Treasure," I warned.

The limo took off to take us back to the Cosmopolitan. It felt good knowing that when we left to go back to California tomorrow, we would be going back as husband and wife. I could feel Treasure rubbing herself against me in the limo. I was ready to fuck her ass all up and in this limo.

"Don't play with a nigga's dick unless you ready to take these backshots and have my kid coming out of you in the next nine months," I warned Treasure. Ever since Treasure gave me her virginity (I am not counting Blach raping her because I'm the only man she gave it to willingly. Therefore, I took her virginity) we had been fucking like animals in the penthouse suite, and I was out of condoms. I should have had the limo driver stop at a Walgreens to get some condoms, but I just wanted to get back to the hotel and celebrate our wedding day.

"Do you like that, bae?" Treasure asked as she pulled my long, thick rod out of my pants and started massaging it in her hands. I was about to be putty in her hands and fuck her all up and down this fucking limo.

Before I could even say anything, she took all of me in her mouth and started pleasuring me. I have had tons of blow jobs, but the way Treasure was pleasuring me put all of the previous women to shame. I felt my eyes start to roll to the back of my head.

"Awww fuck, Treasure! You making me feel like a bitch!" I yelled and ended up cumming in her mouth.

Treasure wasn't done with me yet though. She pulled her red dress up and hopped on my dick before I could say anything. This was the first time I was feeling her wet love box raw, and I knew that I would never use condoms with Treasure again. She started bouncing up and down on my dick. The limo was moving, and I made sure to hold on to her so she wouldn't fall.

"Klayton, this dick is going to make my ass crazy. I can't get enough of you," Treasure whispered. Her love box sounded like stirring macaroni and cheese, and I was two seconds from tapping out on her ass.

"Treasure Milan Jackson, this pussy is mine. I will go on a murder spree over this fucking pussy," I warned her. Her walls were so tight, I knew I was about to bust all of my kids inside of her. Treasure was definitely going to have all of my babies even though I wasn't trying to get her pregnant right now.

"I'm cumming," Treasure moaned, and I was thankful because I wasn't going to last much longer inside of her.

"Fuck, I'm about to bust too." I let all of my kids loose inside of her and pulled her off of me. Treasure's face looked flushed. That's what good dick would do to you.

"I'm going to go and get a plan B later on," Treasure whispered, and I was in full agreeance. Now was not the time for us to have a baby of our own when she needed to get custody of her daughter from her parents.

"When we get back to the room, I will see if the butler for our room can pick up a Plan B pill for us, bae," I agreed, and Treasure looked offended. I wasn't sure what I said that was wrong, but I knew I pissed my wife off.

"I didn't expect you to agree so easily. Would it have been a problem if I did get pregnant, Klayton?" Treasure asked quietly.

"Treasure, I want to have an entire football team with you, but now is not the time. Kamar is out there lurking. It's bad enough that he knows about you and can use you as a weakness against me. Then the fact remains that we need to get custody of Genesis. I know you and your parents had an agreement to let them raise her, but baby girl, you got a real ass nigga in your life now that is going to force you to step up to the plate and be the mother that Genesis needs. You don't want Genesis to grow up feeling rejected, wondering why you never raised her and ended up taking care of the kids that you are going to have with me. Every child wants the love of their parents, and it is easier to tell Genesis now while she is little, and you can still raise her than when she gets older and it's harder for you guys to have a relationship."

I love Treasure, but she is still a bit immature. I was going to help her grow up and become the woman that I knew that she was fully capable of being, and it wasn't a matter of trying to change her personality. I accept and love Treasure for who she is, but I was going to help her become even better than she is now.

"I know you are right, Klayton, but I couldn't help but feel some type of way like you didn't want me to have your baby," Treasure whispered. I couldn't wait for the day that she carried my seed, but now was not the time. It is rare to find a woman that doesn't have rent-a-center pussy and has a good head on her shoulders.

"When the time is right, I'm going to keep you pregnant with my damn seed. I also want us to get used to being married and having time as a married couple first. Children change things and while we have Danielle and Genesis, we need to take our time because we do have a blended family," I explained.

"I'm sorry I jumped to conclusions and assumed things. It just made me feel bad like you didn't want me to have your child. Now that I know and heard your reasoning, I understand," Treasure admitted.

I also wanted to be sure that when we did have a child, Treasure didn't need to be on her medication and hadn't had any episodes for a while. That was something I wasn't going to say to her though and chance pissing her off.

"I love you, Treasure and if I never saw you carrying my seed, I never would have married you. Granted, I don't want to use condoms, so I'm going to have to pull out. Maybe we can go to the doctor and get you on birth control until we are ready to go half on a baby. There is just too much going on for us to think about it right now, and you are finishing school. I want you to reach your goals and start that private practice that you want. You mean so much to me, Treasure. You will never have to doubt how I feel about you."

23

KAMAR

I decided to go back to California and fly to San Antonio. No one would think to look for me here, and Klayton didn't have any niggas out here. If I went back to Philly or New York, those would be the first two places that Klayton would think to look for me. The hard part has been trying to outsmart Klayton and stay hidden so he wouldn't be able to find me. Luckily, I had cousins on my mother's side of the family that I could hide out with. I decided to go to Charlotte's house until I figured out my next move. Charlotte was one of those scheming, nasty hoe ass broads that fucked their way for a come up. That factor worked in my favor because she used to be married to one of the Jackson brothers, and I could use her as a pawn to get what I wanted.

"It is nice of you to come into town, Kamar. I haven't seen you in years, so what brings you to see me?' Charlotte asked curiously with a hand on her hip.

I knew that Charlotte had gotten divorced from Trayce Jackson a few years ago because she was keeping it in the family on some hoe shit. It looked like she had been doing well for herself because she was now working as a nurse and her nigga, Dwight, sat on the couch drinking a beer with his fat ass beer gut. Charlotte definitely downgraded from her ex-husband, but I knew she was the person to see. See, I knew that she was married to Klayton's brother, and she had fucked Klayton a long time ago. Now I was going to see if I could get her on the winning team to help bring Klayton down.

"I was wondering if I could talk to you for a minute, Charlotte. In private of course," I grinned.

Charlotte and I are first-cousins on my mother's side of the family, but we were never particularly close growing up. I usually would see her once a year during the holidays, but we always tried to keep in contact even if that was just to exchange holiday cards. I did talk to her right before I started planning to take Klayton down and learned from her that Trayce passed the business down to Klayton. I was hoping to play on the fact that she had some hatred for Klayton and Trayce for how they treated her.

"Let's go to my room and we can talk." Charlotte gestured to me to go to her room. Dwight's sloppy ass called himself getting up and getting in between us.

"You aren't going anywhere with my woman, jackass. For all I know, you aren't her damn cousin." Dwight pointed his finger in my face. I clocked his ass with a two-piece in the face and he fell into the table with glass shattering everywhere.

"Fuck you, Dwight. Just so you know, Charlotte really is my cousin, but I might make her suck my dick just to spite your ass." I spit on Dwight and walked past Charlotte into her bedroom.

"What did you do that for, Mar? First, you show up out of the fucking blue expecting me to take you in until you figure out a way to get out of the bullshit you got yourself into, and now you punch my nigga in the face," Charlotte complained as she sat on the bed.

Her ample breasts bounced in the tank top she was wearing, and I could tell she wasn't wearing a bra. For some reason, I felt my dick get hard even though I knew that we were related. I never understood why family can't fuck with family. Granted Charlotte has been run through more like a choo choo train, but as long as I could hit that shit, I had no problem with it.

"Charlotte, we are family, and I do need your help. Your titties are about to fall out and unless you want me sucking on one of 'em, you better put 'em away," I winked, knowing she wasn't going to be offended. Hell, I was only treating her like that whore that she was. I shouldn't be attracted to my cousin but hell, I couldn't help myself.

"Nigga, don't think I don't see that erection you got. Now, what do you want?" Charlotte asked impatiently.

"So, I know a way we can get revenge on your ex-husband and his brother, but I'm going to need your help," I started.

Charlotte's eyes lit up and I could tell she wanted to know more. "I told you all that I knew before you went on this suicide mission to take Klayton down. I told you then I didn't want any parts of it, and I don't want any parts of it now. I was lucky to get away with my life after all that I did to Trayce." Charlotte looked at me.

"Come on, Charlotte. I never took you for being a coward. Look at how you are living now and how you have downgraded since your divorce. You should be living in the lap of luxury, but you are out here having to work a fucking job now. Trayce at least could have given you more in the divorce. So what if you were cheating on him? Niggas cheat on their women all of the time and women take them back. This is your chance to get revenge on Klayton and Trayce. Once I come up, you know I'm going to break you off with your fair share," I lied. I had no intention of giving Charlotte shit, but I wanted to do whatever I had to do to get her to go along with the program.

"How much are we talking?" Charlotte folded her arms and her voluptuous breasts were popping out. I had to tell myself to stay focused before I ended up fucking the shit out of my own cousin.

"I will give you one hundred thousand dollars—"

"Nigga, you got to be joking. Trayce and Klayton are killing the game and billionaires many times over. If you think I'm going to help you and take such a small cut, you got me busted." Charlotte shook her head. I just knew that I was going to have to kill this bitch. I would off her ass as soon as I got what I wanted from her.

"I was just joking to make sure you were on your toes. I will give you ten million once the mission is accomplished. Now if that isn't fair, I don't know what is," I negotiated.

I could tell Charlotte was on the fence, which was why I hadn't told her what the plan was so far. I needed to be sure that she wasn't going to flip on me. A part of me thinks that she is still in love with Trayce, but I needed her to understand that she wasn't even a thought in his mind anymore.

"What do I have to do for ten million? Hell, I would be able to live the good life again, which I miss. I had to pawn all of the bags that I had from my marriage to help pay the rent because Dwight's ass is useless. The only thing he is good for is dick," Charlotte vented to me. I decided to play on her emotions and get her to see things my way.

"All you need to help me do is hit the Jacksons, especially Klayton, where it hurts. See, I tried to kill him and his girlfriend, Treasure, and that failed miserably. I came close to killing Treasure, but she ended up in a coma and survived."

Charlotte frowned. "That nigga Klayton has a girlfriend? Klayton has never been the type of nigga to settle down, although he was sprung over that Shae bitch. I wonder what the hell happened to her."

"Why does it matter unless you have feelings for Klayton? I thought you guys were just fuck buddies because you wanted to marry Trayce back in the day." My cousin really is a slut bucket, and she put the phrase 'keeping it all in the family' to good use.

"Klayton isn't the type to settle down. He's a hoe, and he had better dick than Trayce. Trayce was the type that would make love to me, but Klayton would give me that rough, hair pulling sex that I liked. Then I was fucking Akir, and he had that dick that would have your toes curling, but he is dead and gone." Charlotte started lowering her fingers to her pussy, and I could tell she was turned on by the thought of her fucking either of the brothers again.

"Listen, I need you to focus. It is well worth your while to consider my plan because your entire life will change. You won't be living in a dump anymore, and you can go back to living the wealthy lifestyle that you deserve. The thing is, I need to know whether you are all in or not." I stared at Charlotte.

"Does it make me a bad person if I'm considering your offer?" Charlotte asked.

"Nope, both of those niggas are out there living their best life. They sure aren't thinking about you. You should be feeling some type of way that they discarded you like a piece of trash and they out there living the good life. This is your time to shine and get some revenge on them. Wouldn't it be nice to know that you helped with their demise, and we will benefit from the fruits of their labor?"

I knew I was starting to get my point across, and it looked like my plan just might be working. I should have just gone with this idea from the jump instead of trying to convince Pablo's ass to try to help. Soon, he would be bowing down and kissing my feet once I got rid of the Jackson brothers, especially Klayton. I was going to bring that nigga to his knees if that was the last thing that I did.

"You have a point. I still have some love for Trayce, but I hate Klayton. Can we kill Klayton and leave Trayce alone?" Charlotte asked.

"Come on and use your brain for a second. We have to get rid of all of the brothers in order to take over. What good is it to kill Klayton then Trayce or Kobe ends up running shit?" I asked.

"What kind of plan do you have to get rid of them because it looks like you are a one-person army? It's going to be hard enough for us to plot and scheme against the Jacksons. I learned the hard way that they are a force to be reckoned with." Charlotte stared at me.

"Come on, Charlotte, you aren't dealing with a newbie. Did I not build my own empire from scratch?" I asked her.

"You fail to mention that Pablo did most of the work in building that shit. You know you sat back and let him do all of the legwork. He was the brains of that fucking operation, so don't give yourself too much credit."

"That might be true, but I was the one that came up with the plan, so why should I have to put in any unnecessary work when I had a crew? Before you even ask, I'm not going to leave you hanging because there is no way you can pull this off on your own. In fact, this plan involves several steps and the first involves his girlfriend, Treasure. If we execute this plan, this will bring him to his knees, but I need your help. Now are you in or are you out?" I asked impatiently.

Charlotte sat there for a moment deep in thought. I prayed that she made the right decision because I didn't have a plan C if she refused to help me. I would be stuck starting over again and that was simply not an option. Charlotte stared at me and gave me a devious smile.

"Let me know what the plan is. I am all in."

24

TREASURE

It was a couple of days later, and Klayton and I came back from our Vegas trip yesterday. It was just what I needed to get my mind off of things. I couldn't believe that I really went and married the man of my dreams. Klayton isn't perfect and he made a mistake, but I knew he was sincere in his apology. I didn't want to be weak and tolerate cheating, but even I started to recognize that he wasn't making smart decisions while I was in that coma. Besides, he paid more than his fair share when I almost shot his daughter, and I felt bad about that incident.

"Hey, bae, come to the garage for a second."

Klayton's sexy ass walked into the room, and I could feel myself getting aroused. How did I get so lucky to land him? I knew that I was still immature, spoiled and had things to work on, yet Klayton still chose to be with me, so I knew I needed to fully let go of the club incident.

"What is going on?" I asked curiously. I got up and saw Klayton licking his lips at me, and I blushed. My breasts were spilling out of my purple tank top. If I had my way, Klayton and I would be going rounds again.

"I got a surprise for you, and I want to give you the world."

Klayton grabbed my hand and led me towards the garage. He opened it, and I walked inside to see a purple ribbon on top of a brand-new blue Porsche Panamera, my dream car. I stood there in shock because I couldn't believe Klayton did this for me.

"Bae, you didn't even have to—"

"This is your wedding present from me. Thank you for marrying me, Treasure. I promise to make you the happiest woman in the world. You don't ever have to worry about any of these hoes out here because the only woman that can get this pipe is you." Klayton stared at me lovingly, and I had tears in my eyes.

"Klayton, I don't even deserve this. Why would you even want to marry me after what happened to Danielle?" I asked curiously.

Klayton cupped my face in his hands and looked into my eyes. "We both know we were at fault for what happened, Treasure. I'm so sorry that I hurt you and even put you in that position. I can't take back what happened in the past, but I can promise you on my life that I will never cheat on you again and risk what we have. I didn't know what love was until I met you and nothing is worth losing that. I actually spoke to Sparkle, the CPS worker. She checked out my house before we went to Vegas and approved of how I have the guns locked up and measures I made to ensure Danielle's and Genesis's safety. She also saw the ramp I made for Genesis so she can get around easily when she comes over," Klayton explained, and I had tears in my eyes. Klayton might have had selfish ways in the past, but he definitely wasn't selfish with me. He made sure to take care of things for me before I even asked him, and I knew this was the only man out there for me.

"I'm sorry for reacting off of my emotions, Klayton. I could have reacted differently and when I lashed out at you before, it was because I couldn't deal with the guilt from my role in the incident. How can you forgive me so easily?" I asked curiously.

"If this was the old Klayton, I would have held a grudge for a while and might not have forgiven you. I have grown and matured, and I know that we could have handled that differently. It is easy for me to forgive you because Danielle wasn't hurt, and I was just as much at fault as you were with that situation. I only want you to promise me one thing, Treasure." Klayton stared at me expectantly.

"What is that?" I would give almost anything to make sure Klayton was happy. He has done so much for me without asking for a damn thing. I knew I was going to get myself together, not for him, Genesis or my parents, but for myself because that is what they all would want.

"I want you to start taking your medication again and go back to counseling regularly. I want to see you living your best life, Treasure. You can only do that if you have your medical condition under control. I want you to know that I don't judge you for it and at your age, you have gone through more than many grown women have. I love all of you, Treasure Milan Jackson. And whatever bumps in the road come our way, we can get through them together. I don't look at you any differently than before I knew you were diagnosed with schizophrenia," Klayton reassured me. This man has his flaws, but I felt like he was made just for me.

"Thank you for accepting all of me, Klayton, flaws and all. I promise you I'm going to work on getting my life together. Can I take this baby for a test spin? I really want to go visit my parents and tell them we got married," I squealed in excitement. I don't even know how or when Klayton ordered this car for me, but I was learning not to underestimate Klayton. When his mind was made up, he made things happen.

Klayton kissed me passionately and I got lost in the kiss for a moment. "Give me a minute, and I will come with you. I want to be sure you are safe because Kamar's snake ass is still in hiding. and I don't want you going out alone. I almost lost you once. I won't lose you again."

"I love you too. You can't always be with me, especially when I go back and start my clinicals." I caressed Klayton's face.

I understood his fear because I felt the same way about him. At the same time, I knew that he wasn't going to change up his lifestyle just because he fell in love with me. I knew from jump that I was dealing with a street nigga, and I needed to accept him as he is. It didn't mean that I wasn't scared because everyday I thought about how I would handle it if I got that call saying my husband was murdered.

"I know. I'm going to have my people following you around. My brother, Kobe, volunteered to help keep an eye on you along with some security I hired because I refuse to play with your life, and he knows how I feel about you," Klayton explained. I understood where he was coming from. I decided to change the subject because I knew I wouldn't change his mind.

"When do you plan to tell your family that we got married?" I asked Klayton.

"I plan to tell them the next time I go to Trayce's house. The one thing you won't have to worry about is me keeping you a secret. Are you worried about how Luca will react when he finds out?" Klayton asked.,

"Luca and I aren't on good terms. I love my brother, but he is going to have to get over his shit fit. I cannot continue to live my life in a bubble because that makes him happy, and I am not keeping our marriage a secret. I was hoping to tell my parents today when I went over there and pray everything went well."

"I don't think your parents will have a problem with our marriage. I want to start getting to know Genesis because I'm going to be here to help you with her," Klayton explained. I don't know what other man would have willingly taken on all of the baggage that I had presented.

"I need to talk to my parents about talking to Genesis. We need to tell her soon—" I was interrupted by the doorbell ringing. Who the fuck could that be? No one really knew about Klayton's other house outside of his family. My own family didn't know about this place yet.

"Let me answer that before we leave." Klayton let me go, and I followed him back in the house.

He walked to the door and there was a pretty, red headed female standing at the door. "Klayton, I was hoping to catch you—"

"Who the fuck are you? I'm his wife, Treasure. Do you see this ring he picked out for me in Vegas? You need to state your reason for being here and get ghost because my HUSBAND and I have things to do and people to see." I quickly pushed myself in front of Klayton so this bitch wouldn't get to see his dick print. I was being petty. Now that I had a taste of Klayton, I wouldn't even allow the next bitch to think she could sample what was mine.

"You must be that crazy bitch, Treasure. My name is Sparkle and I am Danielle's CPS worker, so I suggest you respect me. I would hate for you to be the reason I put her ass in the system," Sparkle's thirsty ass giggled.

I was about to beat her ass. She was not about to abuse her power just because she couldn't have my man. Before I could respond, Klayton spoke up. "Treasure, let me handle this shit. In fact, go in the living room until we are ready to go."

"Nigga, don't dismiss me like I am your little pet. What the fuck is this bitch doing here and why is she so comfortable doing pop-ups?" I complained.

"Sparkle, wait here for a moment. Treasure, come here." Klayton was pissed as he dragged my ass in the living room. He didn't even wait for a response from Sparkle, and I could tell Klayton was about to give me some act right.

"Are you playing my ass, Klayton? Let me know now because my heart is involved, and that bitch is after your damn dick." I was a bit insecure because Sparkle is beautiful as hell and Klayton could have any woman that he wanted. I said that I had let go of him getting dome, but with another beautiful woman in his face, I was definitely feeling insecure.

"I just went and married your ass and bought you a new car. You are living the life that Sparkle wants, Treasure. I have no reason to want to fuck with her. Is she pretty? If I were single, I might let her suck my dick a couple of times and give her the hoe treatment. I'm not single though because I married you. Hell yeah, but she has nothing on you. You are the woman that I fell in love with. I know that I messed up and I have to earn your trust back. This insecure shit you are on isn't cute though, Treasure," Klayton warned me. Before I could say anything else, he stuck two curved fingers in my wet, love box and I gasped.

"K-Klayton, we can't fuck with Sparkle at the door. She might listen to us fuck and—"

"Well if she is going to listen, we should put on one hell of a show then, shall we? She would get the picture that I'm not trying to fuck with her in that kind of way" Klayton shrugged his shoulder. This nigga is bat shit crazy wanting to fuck with someone outside listening to us, but I was low key turned on by Klayton's level of crazy.

"Fuck me, Klayton. Give me the dick please," I begged, and I busted all over his fingers. He pulled them out of my sopping wet vagina and licked his fingers.

"Damn, you taste good, bae. Toot that ass in the air just how I like it," Klayton ordered. I quickly forgot Sparkle was there until I heard her speak up.

"Would you guys like to add one more party to the mix? It has always been my dream to have a threesome and I am bisexual."

25

BRII

Adrian and I are starting to become inseparable. I felt bad because Jonah was dead, and it was becoming easier for me to move on from what we had. I wasn't looking to fall in love right now, but Adrian and I both went through a lot and our pain had bonded us.

"Brii, are you here with me? I see you are physically here with me, but you haven't been paying attention in group. Would you mind sharing with us what is on your mind?" Jonathan, one of the co-therapists, asked.

I couldn't really share what was on my mind because it wasn't exactly appropriate for group therapy. I knew that if I wanted to get out of here anytime soon, I would have to open up in group, but I didn't want to feel like I was being judged. Before I could respond, one of the other counselors walked in the room.

"I apologize for interrupting group, but I need Brii to come to the room for family sessions as soon as this session ends. Someone is here to see her, and it is important."

My mind was racing at who it could be. Ever since I had been admitted, no one had come to visit me, which told me that everyone hated me for what happened. I felt alone and the main source of support that I had was Adrian. I was becoming more attached to him.

"Brii, go ahead and go since time is almost over. Be prepared to be in the hot seat tomorrow," Jonathan warned me. I gratefully got up and went to the room where family sessions are held.

On the way there, I thought about who could be there to see me, and I prayed that I wasn't about to receive any more bad news. I took a deep breath then opened the door. My legs almost gave way when I saw Nikki and Kobe staring at me with a blank look on her face. I guess it was better than dealing with her hating me, but I certainly wasn't expecting her to be here.

"Please come on in, Brii. I know you are surprised, but Nikki and Kobe wanted to see how you are doing. My name is Justine Watkins, and I will be overseeing this session."

"Where are the kids at?" I asked Nikki and Kobe, confused. Maybe someone else was monitoring them, but part of me wanted to see them. I miss Antoinette, Blake, and Leslie more than I could express, and my heart broke every day that we were apart. Yet, I still didn't want to be responsible for raising them and held some resentment towards them. I didn't completely understand it.

"The kids are at Trayce's house. Nikki and I discussed it, and we are not going to bring them to see you until we are certain that you are stable. We have to put their best interests first," Kobe explained, and I could feel the anger start to come out of me.

I pointed a finger in Kobe's face. "Listen, nigga. I would never put any of the kids in danger. I hate how you and Nikki are on your high horse trying to judge me when neither of you understand what the hell I have been through."

"You better get your finger out of my husband's face before I snap the bitch off!" Nikki yelled, and she got up in got in my face.

"Ladies! Sit down! There will not be any violence, or I will end this session immediately. I understand this is a volatile situation that has been hard on all of you, but we are going to talk this out," Justine insisted, and Kobe had gotten in between us. Nikki reluctantly sat down, but she was pissed off.

Hell, how the hell did she think I felt knowing that my actions hurt the kids even though that wasn't my intent? It was bad enough that I was dealing with the guilt stemming from Jonah's death, but I felt like being in front of Nikki and Jonah was only putting me in another place of judgment.

"Brii, please explain what had you upset about what Kobe said. Personally, I find it admirable that they are taking care of your kids and putting their needs first because the children are innocent, and someone has to speak for them," Justine replied and took a sip of water.

"I love Antoinette, Blake, and Leslie with everything in me, and it felt like they were judging me like I'm a crazy person because of what I did. I know my actions were crazy, but I wasn't thinking from a rational place—"

"How could you be so selfish, Brii? Jonah loved you more than life itself and your actions fucked things up for everyone, including the kids. I understand that you were hurt because of what had happened to you, but we could have gotten through it together."

"Nikki, Jonah found out what Kamar did to me the wrong way, but what was his excuse after he found out? He wasn't there for me at all and distanced himself from me. Do you know how hard it was for me to cope with the fact that he date raped my ass, and no one was there for me? I wish I could go back and stop myself from taking those pills, but I wasn't myself and I'm sorry I hurt you. I'm sorry I hurt Jonah and caused his death. For the rest of my life, I have to live with the fact that I caused his death. I was not in a good place—"

"You were fucking selfish, Brii, and only thought of yourself! You were not the first female to get date raped, and you won't be the last. Hell, Treasure handled what happened to her better than you did, and she was younger! I fucking hate you for what you did to the entire crew! How the hell am I supposed to explain this to Leslie when he gets older? Hell, Jonah was the only father figure that Antoinette and Blake know and now he is gone. Did you even think how his death would affect them considering how many people they lost in their lifetime? Kobe and I have enrolled them in play therapy because I know they are going to have abandonment issues. I am working on filing for full custody of them because you are incapable of raising them, Brii, and you don't deserve them." Nikki pointed her finger in my face.

Tears slid down my cheek. It was enough to break me. I didn't expect things to go the way that they did, and Nikki was right. I was no better to Antoinette and Brii than my mother the crackhead was, and I knew what the right thing to do was. This was going to break my heart, but for once I had to do what was best for the kids and not be selfish. I love them, but I was a mere shell of myself, and if I wasn't good for myself then I certainly wasn't capable of raising children.

"Let me stop you guys right here for a second. Brii, I will let you respond in a second, but I wanted to interject here. Nikki, it sounds like you are hurt by Brii taking those pills. I want you to know that when people decide to commit suicide, they aren't capable of thinking from a rational place. It sounds like you are hurt because she was incapable of making a better decision. At that moment, Brii was in so much emotional pain that she couldn't get past that. It is unfair to punish her for something she was incapable of giving. The same way you point out how the kids were abandoned, that was how she felt when Jonah wasn't there for her in her weakest moment. Did I summarize that correctly, Brii?" Justine asked.

I was grateful Justine spoke up at that moment because I needed an extra moment to get myself together. "Nikki, you are right. I'm very selfish, and I don't deserve the kids. I don't even want to put you through a legal fight for them. I love them enough to do the best thing for them and that is to sign my legal rights over. You and Kobe are amazing, and I can understand why you guys hate me. There is no excuse for what I did, and I can't give you an explanation other than I'm sorry. If you guys come back to visit me, I will sign custody over on your next visit, or we can do this when I get out of the hospital. I just don't want to create more of an inconvenience in your life," I started sobbing and there wasn't a dry eye in the room. Even Justine was crying.

"I'm hurt, Brii, because you know how much I love you. It is hard for me to understand that you were willing to let Kamar win by trying to take your own life. You know I would be there for you and Ro too. Do you understand that Kobe and I literally saw Jonah shoot himself in the head right in front of us? Our lives are forever changed from seeing that. Sometimes I have nightmares from replaying that in my head, and I have started to go to counseling to deal with that. My therapist says that I have PTSD. I haven't had sex with my own husband in the last two weeks. Your drama has affected all of us, Brii, even if that wasn't what you intended. I still love you, yet part of me hates you for what you did to us," Nikki cried, and I watched Kobe rub her back.

Honestly, I was jealous of Nikki and Kobe's relationship. I know that they were going through a hard time, but I envied the love that they shared, and I wanted to find my happiness again. Maybe my karma was going to be the fact that I ended up alone and having to live with the poor choices that I made.

"Nikki, please tell me more about the day you watched Jonah shoot himself in the head. Why is it that you are mad at Brii for trying to kill herself, but you appear to have more sympathy for Jonah? I'm not saying you shouldn't feel sad about losing Jonah, but they both were in a place of pain and couldn't cope with their problems."

"What makes me not hate Jonah is the fact that he had to walk in the house and find Brii's body. I hate that Brii was so weak that she couldn't call one of us. She knows I would have dropped everything to be there for her. Even if Jonah wasn't there for her like he should have been, she had a support system. Brii chose not to use it and take the selfish way out, so it is harder for me to feel bad for her. If she didn't take the pills, none of this would have happened. Maybe Brii and Jonah would have still had marital issues, but they could have gotten counseling and dealt with that. Brii's suicide attempt directly lead to Jonah taking his life." Nikki stared at me.

"Kobe, how do you feel about everything? I notice that you have been really quiet during the session," Justine remarked.

"I don't hate Brii. I feel like she was in a really bad place, and she didn't anticipate all that happened, but I don't hate her. I'm also conflicted because I know Nikki feels some type of way, but I really just want us to fix this the best that we can. I do support getting custody of the kids, but I would never want to cut Brii out of the picture because the kids will still need her to be a part of their lives. This is just a really rough situation on all of us, but know that we still care about you, Brii."

26

KLAYTON

I couldn't believe Sparkle offered to do a threesome. If this was the old Klayton, I wouldn't have hesitated to take her up on her offer. The thing was, I had no interest in sharing my wife, even if it was with another woman.

"Listen Ronald fucking McDonald, take your bright ass out of my house because it is not that kind of party. I am not sharing my wife's pussy," I snapped.

Treasure looked shocked and I was tempted to let her beat Sparkle's ass, but I didn't want Sparkle to put Danielle in the system out of spite. Some of these bitches are on some spiteful type of time, and I put nothing past Sparkle. I knew from jump she wanted this dick and if I had met her before Treasure, I might have busted a few nuts down her throat but that certainly wasn't going to be the case now.

"Klayton, is that how you speak to your guest? All I have to do is place one phone call and—" I grabbed Sparkle by her neck and threw her ass outside on the front yard.

"Go ahead and call the police about me putting my hands on you. I have cameras all over this property showing you being a peeping tom, watching me about to fuck my wife. I doubt they would find that appropriate behavior if I reported your ass to your supervisor. Oh, and by the way, my phone was on record, so I recorded what you said about having a threesome. I highly suggest you leave me and my wife alone, especially since you already checked off that I was in the clear and could have custody of my daughter again. If you even think of trying to take my daughter from me, I promise you, your family that lives on 123rd and Avalon will be floating in the Pacific Ocean. That is a fucking promise and not a threat." I walked away from her and saw Treasure right behind me.

I locked the front door up and put the security system on since Treasure and I were about to leave. We would finish fucking later, but I knew Treasure wanted to go give her parents the news that we had gotten married.

"Do you think Sparkle is going to leave us alone? I don't want you going to jail, Klayton. She isn't worth it." Treasure looked worried, and I bent down to meet her at eye level.

"Sparkle knows not to mess with us anymore. Trust me, she doesn't want this fucking smoke. Let's go to your parent's house, so I can come back and stick my stick in your fucking crease," I smirked. I couldn't get enough of being inside Treasure and there wasn't another woman out there that could compare to her.

"I love you, Klayton, and I don't want to lose you." Treasure looked sad and it broke my heart. I would protect this woman and keep her from harm for the rest of her life. I would do everything I could to keep a smile on her face, and I didn't want Treasure worrying about me.

"You don't have to worry about a thing. I just need you to hang in there with a nigga because this will all be over with soon. I'm going to focus on finding Kamar and killing his ass and anyone that is working with him After that drama is settled, I promise you things will calm down, Treasure. Just hang in there with a real nigga," I pleaded.

Treasure smiled and we went and got in her brand-new car. I tossed her the keys, and she started driving to her parents' house.

Twenty minutes later, we pulled up to their home, and I squeezed Treasure's hand.

"I'm here with you every step of the way, regardless what happens, bae," I reassured her.

"I love you, Klayton," Treasure reassured me.

We finally got out of the car. Treasure pulled out a house key that she had and opened the front door. It was quiet when we walked in and walked to the kitchen. Hope was in the kitchen with Genesis and Gigi's ass. If that wasn't some damn bullshit, I just knew Treasure was going to beat her ass. I was disappointed in Treasure for fighting in front of her daughter because she needed to set a better example for her. I grabbed Genesis and got her out of the room because she didn't need to see this shit go down and then went back to the kitchen.

"Oh hell naw, mom! What is that bitch doing here?" Treasure pointed at Gigi.

"Who the hell are you calling a bitch?" Gigi stared at Treasure before looking at me and then looking away. A lightbulb must have gone off in her head, and she looked like she was about to piss her pants.

"Listen, little girl, you don't want these fucking problems. I don't want your nigga. He was the one that cheated on you. He owed you loyalty, not me. What happened was me being a single woman at a night club and it didn't go beyond me biting his dick because he called me your name. I don't owe you an explanation, so you're lucky that I'm giving you one."

"Bitch, you are not good enough for my brother with your hoe ass!" That was the last thing Treasure said before Gigi slapped the shit out of Treasure, and I quickly stepped in the middle. This situation was messy as hell.

"Why did you put your hands on my daughter, Gigi?" Hope cried.

"Listen, this was a bad idea. I don't know why I let Giovanni talk me into staying here. I will get my ass a hotel, I'm out."

Gigi started to walk away, but Treasure grabbed her by her hair and dragged her to the ground. Treasure transformed into the Incredible Hulk because she was throwing haymakers, and Gigi was giving back as good as she got.

"Hope, get Gigi! I got Treasure's little ass!" I yelled. I picked her little ass body off of the ground and pressed my body against hers to where she couldn't get loose.

"Let me fucking go, Klayton, and beat her ass for sucking your dick!" Treasure's crazy ass yelled.

"Stop it or I'm going to cancel your dick appointment later, Treasure. You flipped out on that girl when she didn't even know about you. What happened was all my fault and you out here looking goofy trying to check her when she hasn't even been trying to come for me since the incident," I whispered.

"Hope, let me go so I can leave," Gigi stated calmly.

"No, we are going to sit down and talk about this," Hope sounded delusional because Treasure is in crazy mode. There is no reasoning with her when she gets this way.

Treasure waved her ring finger at Gigi. "This wasn't the way that I wanted to make this announcement, but Klayton and I are married!"

Hope and Gigi stared at Treasure's ring finger. I looked at Gigi to see if I could sense any emotion either way, and it didn't look like she cared. "Congratulations to both of y'all. I don't even want, Klayton. I never would have gone there with him that night if I knew he wasn't single. I'm not built that way. You don't have to like me, but you are going to respect me," Gigi bossed up on her.

"Listen, Gigi. I like you, but this is my daughter. If I have to choose then my loyalty will always ride with her. Treasure, you have to understand that wasn't Gigi's fault what happened because she had no way to know Klayton was with you. Klayton, you better fix this shit, especially since you went and married my daughter. Hell, I wanted to be there to see her get married." Hope looked devastated and I felt bad.

"When things settle down, Treasure and I will have a big ceremony because she deserves better than getting married with fake Elvis in Vegas. I love Treasure, and I will never fuck up like that again.

You can trust me with your daughter's life and her heart" I reassured Hope, although I could see there was a small shadow of doubt.

"Gigi, I need you to be honest with me, and I won't take it the wrong way. Do you have any sort of romantic feelings for my husband?" Treasure asked with her arms folded across her breasts. I never understood why women ask questions to stuff that they really didn't want the answer to and then when you're brutally honest with them, they flip out.

"Hell no, Treasure. Trust me, I am not on no scorned woman shit. If anything, I am in love with Luca. And before any of you guys say shit, understand that I didn't know Klayton and Luca had any bad blood or ties between them at the time. I never would have gone there with Klayton had I known otherwise. I was just there for a night out to unwind." Gigi looked sincere, and I definitely believed her.

"I apologize, Gigi."

"Why are you apologizing to her, Klayton?" Treasure had an attitude.

"I'm apologizing because as a man, I created this situation and should have made better decisions that night. I can't take back what happened, but I'm trying to fix it. Now, are you Luca's girlfriend?" I asked, confused.

"Ex-girlfriend. I doubt we will get back together because I will not allow a man to disrespect me. The club incident happened, but it happened well before Luca and I made things official. I am in love with Luca and that is the only man that I want to be with. I refuse to kiss his ass, and he has really been acting an ass lately." Gigi rolled her eyes.

"Honey, I need you to be patient with Luca. I am mad at my son right now, but we can't give up on him. He needs to get into counseling and work on himself before you can even try to work things out with him. You are in love with him and I know it is hard when you have a broken heart, but things will work itself out with you two," Hope tried reassuring Gigi, and I saw some tears slide down her face.

"The one time I let another nigga in emotionally, he breaks my heart, but I will be fine. I will be out of your way soon. I wish you guys the best of luck and congratulations on your wedding. I hope you guys can be happy together." Gigi got up and walked out of the room. You could hear a pin drop in the room, and this was the last way that I thought things would go today.

"She really is in love with my brother. Too bad Luca is a complete fuck up." Treasure rolled her eyes.

"Treasure! I know Luca messed up with how he treated you at the funeral, but I am begging you to forgive him. Forgiveness is for yourself and not for other people," Hope begged.

"We will see. I need time to get over what he said to me. He triggered me and—"

"Are you taking your medication? I'm worried about you, especially with you deciding to get married the way you did. It is not good to react based off of emotions and—"

"Mom, I'm fine. Klayton is the man that I love and I'm going to spend the rest of my life with. Klayton messed up, but he has really been trying to make things right. Hell, we got back, and he has a ramp installed for Genesis at his house and an entire room decorated and ready for her. He made a mistake, but I'm willing to ride for him." I felt like I was the luckiest man in the world because of the love that Treasure has for me. I was determined to show her that I would protect her heart.

"I know that what we did was last minute, Mrs. Glover, but I can reassure you that I'm going to take good care of your daughter. Life is too short to be unhappy, and I couldn't bare the thought of coming back to LA and Treasure wasn't my wife. We will plan a fancy ceremony, so you can see me marry Treasure, and money will not be an issue. I will also make sure she is taking her medication and finishes her degree. I also wanted to talk to you about us changing the custody arrangement for Genesis."

Hope looked at me with admiration in her eyes. "I can certainly see why you married him, baby girl. All I want is your happiness. I just needed for you to be sure you were ready for marriage. Marriage is a lifelong commitment, baby. You can't threaten to divorce Klayton just because you get in an argument and don't get your way. Treasure, how do you feel about taking custody of Genesis? My concern is you aren't ready because raising a child isn't something that you do part-time. You have to be a full-time parent, especially when things get hard. I feel bad that I took your option to choose away from you and if you need me to raise her, I'm ok with that. Once we tell her you are her mother, that is something that can't be undone." I could understand why Hope had concerns and it was time for Treasure to put her big girl panties on.

"If I'm woman enough to get married and enter adulthood, I need to be woman enough to step up to the plate and raise my child. Where is dad at, mom?" Treasure asked curiously.

"He is staying with Luca until he recovers. We are hoping he will be willing to go get some counseling. I told your dad maybe we can get a therapist that can come to the house. He really needs help. I'm worried about your brother," Hope admitted.

"I'm really upset with Luca right now, but I miss when we used to be close. I just wish he would see that him getting shot was a wake-up call to get the help that he needs." Treasure started biting her nails. She only does that when she is really nervous or upset. I was going to do all that I could to encourage her to fix her relationship with Luca. You only get one family and tomorrow is not guaranteed.

"I know what Luca did wasn't right, and I hate to defend that nigga, but he is still your brother. I love you, Treasure, and I can see how much it hurts you to not have a relationship with your brother." I squeezed her hand.

"Klayton, he was trying to force me to choose between you guys. I refuse to allow my brother to control me anymore. I'm in love with you, but I honestly don't think he will accept our marriage."

I never wanted Treasure to have to choose between us. Maybe I should have thought things through before marrying her impulsively. There were a lot of issues that we needed to work through as a family. I don't know if I could live with it if Luca disowned Treasure for following her heart. Hope must have noticed that I was worried, and she spoke up.

"I don't want you guys to worry about Luca because your father and I are going to continue trying to encourage him to get help. He is also being stubborn because he is in love with Gigi—"

Gigi had walked back in the room and none of us noticed her because we were too caught up in this conversation. "I put Genesis down for a nap. I couldn't help but overhear what you guys said about Luca, and I don't want to overstep my bounds. I am in love with him, and he is trying to push me away. When I went to the hospital to visit him after I found out that he got shot, we got in a bad argument because of the club incident. I have never been the type of woman to allow a man to disrespect me, and Luca's words really hurt me. Now that I think about it, I feel like Luca was pushing me away," Gigi explained, and her explanation made sense. There would have been no reason for Luca to get has mad as he did if Gigi truly was single at the time. How the hell would I know? I wasn't clocking her pussy.

"Gigi, Luca really hasn't been himself the last three years, and AJ's death really changed him. I need you to be patient with him because I have seen glimpses of the old Luca when you guys were together. I'm begging you to not give up on him because Luca can't take another heartbreak," Hope begged.

"Listen Gigi. We got off on the wrong foot and part of me is always going to look at you funny because of the club incident. But if you are truly going to be here for Luca, you need to be all in. I will not tolerate you breaking my brother's heart regardless if my brother and I are on good terms or not. I need to know if you are in or are you out because it is time for this family to start healing."

27

LUCA

I was home from the hospital, and I was going stir crazy because I wasn't used to being a homebody. I was used to burying myself in work, but I didn't have that as a crutch anymore. I miss Gigi and I'm madly in love with her, but I knew that she wasn't fucking with me and rightfully so. I disrespected her when she didn't deserve it and mainly because I was trying to push her away. Why did it feel so bad when I knew that I achieved my goal in pushing her away? My heart was broken, and it was a bad feeling to swallow. I couldn't stop thinking about Gigi. There were a few times I wanted to call her, but I stopped myself from doing so. What compounded things was that I miss my sister, and I knew Treasure wasn't fucking with me for how I treated her at Jonah's funeral.

"Hey, I brought you some dinner, son. You know I can't cook, so I ordered some Mexican food from Uber Eats. It looks like you got a lot on your mind, son. How about we talk over dinner?" My father laid a hand on my shoulder, and I could feel myself on the verge of a mental breakdown. He placed my food on a tray in front of me, but I wasn't hungry.

"Thanks, Dad. You don't have to stay here with me. I can take care of myself. I would rather you be at your house where you can protect our family."

I wanted to push him away so I could wallow in my self-pity. As a man, I'm not too afraid to admit now that I have been severely depressed for the last three years. Depression can manifest its symptoms differently in individuals, and I have truly been miserable. I was starting to see that I needed to make some changes in my life, but that was easier said than done.

"Son, I am not going anywhere and will be here until you get better. You cannot push your family away because we aren't going anywhere—"

The doorbell rang, and my father got up to answer it. I was hoping my mom and Genesis came to visit me, but I was excited when I heard Treasure's voice. That excitement was short lived when I heard that nigga Klayton was with her.

"I wanted to introduce you to my husband, Dad. I just left Mom's house and gave her the news and beat Gigi's ass one good time," I heard Treasure say and I could feel myself starting to get angry. Why would my sister go and marry that nigga after how he cheated on her when she was in a coma? I love my sister, but she was obviously very weak behind Klayton, and I was disappointed.

"Klayton, stay out here while I go check on my brother real quick," Treasure instructed and then opened the door.

"Bitch, you might as well bring that fuck boy in here with you!" I yelled angrily.

"Bitch? Who the fuck are you calling a bitch, Luca?" Treasure yelled. She walked over to the chair I was laying in and slapped the shit out of me.

"Nigga, fuck you say to my wife? What the fuck you not gon' do is disrespect my wife," Klayton busted in the room yelling.

The next thing I heard was the click of a gun, and I knew Klayton had a gun pointed at me. I always knew the nigga was nuts, but he was really about to kill my ass over my sister. Even I had to admit that Klayton was in love with Treasure, but I still felt like he was no good for her.

"Go ahead and shoot my ass fuck boy. Fuck you, bitch! Before she was your wife, she was my sister. And even after she's done being your wife, she's still gonna be my sister. I'ma be the one to dry her tears, hold her to calm her down and make sure she's straight. I always fucking do! And Treasure, I never took your ass for being a weak ass bitch—"

Boom! Boom! Boom!

Three shots went off in rapid succession before I could realize it, and Treasure was screaming at the top of her lungs. "Call her a bitch one more fucking time. I brought her over here so she could see you and you guys could start to work on your relationship. I don't want her to not have you in her life. Treasure needs both of us and you aren't even man enough to recognize that there is room for both of us in her life. I know that you are used to being the man of the house and calling shots with Treasure, but you are playing with my wife now, nigga, and you will not disrespect her. Call her one more bitch, and Treasure will be slow singing and flower bringing."

"Luca, are you ok? Klayton, you really shot Luca, and he just got out of the hospital!" Treasure yelled, and Giovanni ran by my side to check me out. He shot my ass in the fucking foot and it hurt like a motherfucker right now, but I wasn't going to act like a punk in front of Klayton.

"I bet you Luca won't disrespect you again! You are my wife, and I won't let anyone play with you. I'm not sorry for shooting Luca and if he disrespects you again, we will all be attending a fucking funeral. You can be mad at me if you want to, Treasure, but I wouldn't be a man if I didn't defend my wife." Klayton held her in his arms and it made me sick. Not only did I have to cope with my sister falling in love, but I had to deal with my sister cavorting with the enemy.

"Luca, your ass is dead ass wrong. Why can't you be happy for your sister?" My dad fussed. I saw him pick up the phone, and I assumed he was going to have the hood doctor take a look at my foot.

"Treasure, why did you marry him? This nigga is the fucking enemy, man! How could you pick him over your brother? Ever since we were little, I always wanted to make sure you were good. I want you to be happy, just not with Klayton," I insisted, trying to get Treasure to understand where I was coming from. I picked up my tray of food and threw it on the ground. I knew that my behavior was wrong, but I couldn't help how I felt about the situation.

"Luca, I love you but you are acting like a fucking two year old having a temper tantrum. I don't want to have to pick between you and the man that I am in love with. It tears me apart to see that you really want me to pick between you and Klayton. Yes, I married him when he took me to Vegas after you got shot. Klayton made a mistake—"

"Do you really think that nigga is ever going to be faithful to you? What makes you special that Klayton is going to keep his dick in his pants? I don't want you having your heart broken by a nigga that isn't shit."

"Luca! Stop it! Do you really want me to hate you and never speak to you again for the rest of my life? That is what this is coming down to because if you are forcing me to choose then I am choosing my husband. The second that I said I do is the second that he comes first in my life. I feel sorry for you, Luca. You spend so much time pushing your entire family away that you don't understand you need help. I came over to tell you that I need you to get help, so we can work on our relationship. I also wanted you to hear from me that I am married because I am not hiding my marriage just to make you happy. I get after Blach raped me that you became even more overprotective and wanted to keep any harm from coming my way, but you also have to let me live my life. I love you, Luca, even if you don't think I do." Treasure started crying and Klayton got up and wrap his arms around her. Klayton gave me a dirty look, but I didn't care what that nigga thought about me.

"You don't love me, Treasure. If you did, you wouldn't choose another nigga over your brother. Get out. I never want to see you again. As far as I'm concerned, you are dead and gone to me," I stated coldly.

My heart was closed off like a frozen block of ice. I knew that I was hurting my sister, but hell, she was hurting me as well. She wouldn't even listen to what I had to say, and it broke my heart. Fuck Treasure as long as she stayed married to that nigga, especially since she was still taking his side even after he shot me.

"Luca, you are out of line! Apologize to your sister now!" My father screamed and his eyes were bloodshot red. I knew I was being selfish and tearing my family apart, but I couldn't help how I felt.

Treasure was sobbing. Klayton picked her up and carried her out. He looked back at me before he responded. "Like it or not, Treasure is my wife. I wanted to come to you as a man and squash the beef, but I can see you aren't ready for that yet. Get the help that you need, Luca. You are breaking not just your sister's heart, but your niece and your parents too."

Klayton and Treasure finally left, and my father stared at me for a moment. "Luca, you are leaving me no choice but to get your ass locked up in a mental health facility if you choose to not get some counseling. Your selfish ways are tearing the family apart, and I simply can't stand for this any longer."

"How in the hell do you expect me to accept that my sister married Klayton? Everyone knows that I don't fuck with him, but I guess it's fuck Luca's feelings! I wanted to keep Treasure in this little bubble where she would never be interested in a nigga, but that was unrealistic obviously. You are telling that out of every man in this world, she has to marry Klayton Jackson?" I asked and grimaced in pain. Hopefully, the nurse hurried up to look at my foot because I was in a lot of pain.

"You don't have to be best friends with Klayton, but you have to understand that is who Treasure chose to be with. Personally, Klayton is good for her and everyone can see this except for you. You need to mind your business and focus on getting yourself right. It is ok to move on and be happy. AJ would want that for you, and you have a beautiful woman that is making sure your law office stays afloat. She is just waiting for you to get your shit together, Luca. You hurt her with how you talked to her at the hospital. Hope raised you better than to disrespect a woman the way that you did, and Gigi is someone's daughter or sister. How would you like it if Klayton disrespected

Treasure in that manner? I know you would bust a cap in his ass and rightfully so. I love you, and I want you to get your shit together, Luca." The look on my dad's face softened.

Lately, I had been feeling like I was more of a burden on my family than anything. My entire family would be better off if I was gone, but I refused to sound like a pussy and admit how I was feeling to my dad. "I know that I need to do better, dad. When is the nurse coming?" I quickly changed the topic. I didn't like being vulnerable and talk about my feelings.

"You can do better by going to get the help that you need. It is either attend counseling or I start trying to find ways to get you involuntarily committed because you are a danger to yourself and others."

28

TREASURE

"Klayton, you didn't have to shoot Luca!" I yelled at his ass as soon as we got home. I appreciate the fact that my husband had my back, but he went too far when he shot Luca, especially knowing that he had just got out of the damn hospital.

Klayton ignored me and continued smoking his blunt. He blew some smoke in the other direction before he responded.

"Treasure get out my damn man cave. You're disturbing my peace."

I started punching Klayton in the chest and my little hits didn't do much to stop him. He did end up dropping his blunt on the ground though. "Luca was doing too fucking much, but you made the situation worse, Klayton! Hell, my brother fucking disowned me!"

"I get you are in your feelings, Treasure, but I'm not the type of nigga that is going to let another nigga disrespect my wife. The second you said I do, it became my responsibility and my honor to make sure you are protected. Any real man that loves his wife is not gonna let someone call her out of her name. You already know that I have screws loose. Luca got what he deserved when I shot his bitch ass in the foot," Klayton stated nonchalantly.

I love how this man loves me and is willing to protect me. I was stuck between a rock and a hard place. It broke my heart to hear Luca disown me. "I love you, Klayton. You react impulsively, and I don't want you to do things that can get you taken away from me. I'm not trying to take up for Luca, don't get me wrong—"

"I will never be ok with anyone disrespecting you, Treasure. I wasn't ok with it before we got married, and I'm definitely not fucking with that fuck shit now. You don't have to worry about shit because Klayton isn't going anywhere. Do you know it makes me feel like less of a man to watch Luca disrespect you? I can't get down with that and only a fuck nigga would allow that shit to go on." Klayton is definitely an alpha male type of personality and once he has his mind made up about something, you couldn't tell him any different.

"I understand that. All I am saying is I think you took it too far shooting Luca because it is going to be hard for you guys to move forward. Like it or not, he is still my brother, and he has to get used to the fact that you are my husband. You aren't going anywhere anytime soon. I'm not allowing Luca to clock and control my moves anymore because he obviously doesn't care about my feelings, Klayton. Hell, I don't care for Gigi, but I would never tell my brother who he can or can't be with. I wish that he could see that you make me happy, Klayton. To know that he would really disown me over the choice I made hurts," I admitted. I didn't like being stuck between the love of my life and my brother. I love them both in different ways. Klayton is my helpmate and my life partner while my brother is someone that I could never replace. Unfortunately, it looked like I was going to have to choose, and I meant it when I said I would choose my husband.

"There is nothing I wouldn't do to protect you, but I will try to not act as reckless. I don't think clearly when it comes to you, Treasure. I want us to start transitioning to get custody of Genesis. Maybe you can call and offer to take her shopping later on this week. We can bring her over to the house and allow her to start to spend time over here," Klayton suggested and I liked the idea.

There was no better time than the present than to start making things happen. I have talked about getting custody of Genesis, but I knew that Klayton would make me follow through. He really was what I needed in my life. He forces me to be better and not stay stagnant.

"I'm good with that, Klayton. I was thinking to take the upcoming semester off of school and go back in the fall. Hear me out before you object, Klayton." I held my hand up to keep him from interrupting me and then continued. "I need to be able to focus on being a parent to Genesis. It is going to be hard to explain to her that I am her mother and adjust to being a full-time parent. I want to be able to focus on that, go back to counseling and taking my medication again. If I want Luca to treat me like I'm grown, I have to act like I'm grown. I can't counsel others if I'm not making sure that I'm good."

Klayton stared at me for a minute before a smile was on his face. "Treasure, I'm proud of you for trying to recognize and own up to things. I will be here every step of the way and just so you know, you are only taking one semester off. I'm going to stay on your ass because you are going to be an amazing example for our kids."

I looked at Klayton confused. "Our kids, nigga? We don't have any kids together yet."

"The key word is *yet*. I'm going to be the man that raises Genesis and you are going to be the only mother that Danielle knows, so those are our kids. Now enough kee keeing on this emotional shit. When are you gonna ride zaddy's dick?" Klayton grabbed his dick, and I was salivating.

I couldn't get enough of my husband, and his dick game was making me crazy. I grabbed him by the hand and led him to the bedroom, so I could have my way with my husband.

~

"HEY, MOM. HOW ARE YOU DOING?" I greeted my mom the next day.

Klayton had left for the day and told me he was going to handle some shit, aka he was busy trying to find that nigga Kamar and link up with his brothers. I knew he would be gone for a while, so I invited my mother and Genesis to come and check out my new home. I had given her my address and wanted her to see where I was living now and give her a tour of the place. She looked impressed, and Genesis was happily playing with the different toys that Klayton bought for her. When I said my husband is heaven sent, he really is because he made sure to get toys that she could play with due to her disability.

"Klayton went all out for you and Genesis. They don't make many good men like Klayton anymore, so you better hold on to him. I'm happy to see you are finally getting your own happiness. Don't let the situation with Luca stop you because you married Klayton for a reason. Luca will eventually come around." My mom had a smile on her face. Part of me felt like she was kind of delusional, but I knew that she wanted to hold on to hope that her kids would eventually make up and be close again. My heart broke for her because I would kill to have a relationship with my brother again.

"I'm not so sure about that, mom. When I was at his house, he looked at me like I was a common bitch in the streets and said he disowned me. Luca has gotten mad at me before but never to that level where he disrespected me the way that he did. I got on Klayton last night about shooting Luca in the foot," I explained as I took a sip of my coffee. My mom came bearing gifts in the form of Dunkin Donuts coffee and donuts. My greedy ass was ecstatic.

"Luca reacted the way he did because he knows he is losing you, and he doesn't like losing control. Klayton had every right to respond how he did, Treasure, and let me tell you why," my mom replied and folded her hands in her lap.

I was surprised my mother was defending Klayton because at the end of the day, Luca is still her firstborn son. "Klayton could have handled the situation differently is the only thing I'm saying."

"Chile, Luca knows Klayton isn't working with a full fucking deck. If you ask me, Luca kept poking the bear, and he responded. He knew better than to call you out of your name, especially with Klayton being there with you. Luca needs to stop playing the victim. Your father gave him an ultimatum, and I pray he actually gets the help that he needs."

"We both know Luca doesn't do well with ultimatums. How did

he respond?" I asked curiously. The problem was, we could lead a horse to water, but we couldn't make it drink. Luca did not want help and it wouldn't work unless he was ready to receive it.

"Luca told your dad that he is going to try, so let's pray this works out. I just want us all to be a family again." I walked over and gave my mom a hug.

"I promise I will do what I need to do to make that happen, Mom. I love you," I whispered.

I was so grateful to have my mother. Many kids grow up in broken homes with crackhead parents. I was blessed to have a mother and a father that love me. My heart aches for Genesis because her biological father is a piece of shit, but Klayton would definitely make up for that.

"Treasure, I want you to stay away from Luca for now. He needs time to get better and you need to focus on your relationship with Genesis. Speaking of building relationships, let me get Genesis. There is no better time than the present to tell her that you are her mother." My mom got up and went to get Genesis.

I couldn't believe that the moment was finally here, and I was glad my mom was taking the initiative in this situation. It was time to get the ball rolling and tell her so we could start to form a mother-daughter relationship of our own. My mom brought Genesis in the room and sat her next to me.

"Hi, Treasure. I missed you," Genesis whispered shyly.

Genesis is very intelligent for her age, and her fifth birthday is coming up soon. I was going to plan a huge birthday party for her. Genesis deserves nothing but the best, and I was determined to give it to her.

"I love you, Genesis. I have missed you. I have something important to tell you and it is ok if you are confused." I stopped because I wasn't sure on how to tell Genesis. I looked over at my mom for help and she took over.

"You know me as mommy Genesis, but I am not your mommy. I am your grandma. You know Treasure as your sister, right?" My mom whispered slowly.

I could tell Genesis was confused and none of us said anything for a few minutes. We wanted to go at a pace that Genesis was comfortable with.

"Yes, Genesis my sister," Genesis whispered.

I held Genesis hand in mine. "Genesis, I am your mommy. This is your granny, but you can call her whatever makes you feel comfortable for now"

Genesis looked confused. "So, both of you are my mommy?"

"We can both be your mommy if that is what you want. I know you are used to calling me Treasure, but I hope that soon you will be comfortable calling me mommy."

29

KLAYTON

"Yo' I got some news on that fuck nigga, Kamar," Trayce announced.

We were chilling in his man cave and Kobe had come through to shoot the shit with us. Trayce had also called Derek and Trouble to come join us. I was happy because I got to see my daughter, Danielle, earlier and she was playing with Little Jah. I passed the blunt that we had going in rotation. I was in full business mode. The sooner Kamar's ass was dead, the better, so we could all move on with our lives.

"What's the news, nigga?"

"My private investigator tracked Kamar in San Antonio, but guess who lives there and might be helping him with this scheme?" Trayce asked then passed the blunt to Derek.

"Nigga, we don't have time to play Where in the World is Carmen Sandiego. Spill the beans, so I can get on with killing his ass." I was impatient because I was ready for this bullshit to be over with, and Trayce sensed that.

"Remember my ex-wife, Charlotte? Apparently, they are cousins, and they are on their way back here and plotting. I don't know what their next scheme is but be on guard. Damn, maybe we could have avoided this entire situation if I had killed that bitch years ago. I want in on this shit because it is personal. I know you are capable of handling yourself, Klayton, but I want to watch that hoe take her last breath." Trayce looked pissed.

I understood where Trayce was coming from because that was how I felt about Shae when she killed AJ in Coke Gurls Cali. I also knew that I wouldn't be able to talk Trayce out of getting his hands dirty, so I wasn't even going to try arguing with him. It was time to figure out how to draw Kamar's ass out.

"I feel you, bro, so we need to draw Kamar's fuck boy ass out. I wonder if he is planning to use Charlotte as bait. Trayce, you really want in because if so, you will get that bitch out real quick if we use you as bait. The only problem might be Ro won't like that too much."

"What Ro doesn't know won't hurt her, man. Check this, let me call this goofy bitch and convince her to meet up with us." Trayce grabbed his cell phone and called Charlotte.

"Hello? Who is this?" Charlotte answered. We knew this bitch was going to fall for the okie doke because she had no idea that we were on to her bullshit.

"Hey, Char. It's me, Trayce. I was calling you because I have been thinking about you and hoping that life has been treating you well. I haven't stopped thinking about you since the divorce, and I was hoping we could link up soon," Trayce explained. He was lucky Ro wasn't in the room because he sounded a bit too friendly with that whore for my own liking. I know Ro would have acted an ass if she heard this conversation.

"How did you get my number? It is good to hear from you. I'm actually in LA right now for a few days. I'm here for a nursing conference. Maybe we could catch up for old times sake. Well, that is if Rolonda doesn't mind." We could all hear the shade that was being thrown in that comment. I had to put my hand over my mouth to stop from laughing at the stupid bitch. How the hell did she fall for the oldest trick in the book when Trayce hadn't even contacted her in years?

"Ro and I are separated. It turns out that she cheated on me with another nigga, and I'm heartbroken. I was reaching out to see if we could link up and maybe catch up," Trayce suggested.

"That sounds good. When are you available? Maybe we could go back to our favorite Italian restaurant in Beverly Hills and remember all of the good times we had—"

"Naw, that little spot closed down a couple of years ago. How about I pick you up from your hotel tomorrow night say around seven pm, and I pick somewhere for us to go?" Trayce suggested.

"That sounds like a date. I still love you, and I'm sorry I fucked Klayton. I never knew what I had in you until you were gone, and I didn't appreciate you. I really would like it if we could try and take things slow and get to know each other again, Trayce. You know you never really get over your first love," Charlotte cooed, and I was doing my best not to laugh.

"Text me your address, and I will contact you tomorrow when I get to your hotel." Trayce hung up the phone and then we all started laughing.

"Yo', that broad is so fucking dumb! She sounds like she got that fish market pussy ready to bust it open for your ass again!" Trouble yelled.

We all laughed at him except Kobe. Kobe looked like he was deep in thought.

"What's good, Kobe? It looks like you got something on your mind." I encouraged him to speak up.

"Did you guys look into Kamar's connections besides him being connected to Charlotte? I feel like we are missing some information and honestly, that might be a trap Trayce is walking into. Do you really think Charlotte is that dumb or gullible? She is probably telling Kamar right now about that date, and he is getting his plan together. We gotta stay one step ahead of them, and I don't think that date tomorrow is going to be the move." Kobe made a very valid point.

"You reminded me of something, bruh. The PI did tell me is connected with shit on the East Coast and is running shit there. I also heard that this nigga, Pablo Sanchez, is really the mastermind of it and the one putting in all of the work there. I have the PI working to get me as much information as he can on that end," Trayce reported.

"Yo' Trouble, and I can go check this shit out in Philly as soon as you shoot me the information while the rest of you guys stay here and handle shit on this end. There is no need for us all to go when Kamar could end up striking, and we all have families here. Klayton, take little Jah home with you because he can be too much for my wife, Jimmya, to handle," Derek instructed. It did make sense to send them out there and scope out if any of them could be used as bait.

"I wouldn't even target Pablo unless we have to because that could lead to an unnecessary war. I don't fear any man, but we don't need unnecessary east coast west coast beef. What I need to know is if Kamar has any baby momma's, children or where his momma lays her head at because I will kill any of them with no fucks given," I was in savage mode. Normally I don't like killing women, children or pets, but Kamar violated the wrong mothafucking nigga.

"I got some bad news. Kamar has several different baby mamas but he must have them hidden out in the cut somewhere. I did, however, get news of where his mother and his grandmother stay at, so we can target them next," Trayce announced. I appreciate my big brother because he was looking out for me when he really didn't have to. Trayce had gotten out of this life years ago and retired to live the family life with Ro. Now I didn't even ask, but he already had a ton of information for me, so we could start to strategize and come up with a plan.

"Good looking, bruh. You know I'm break you off—"

"Nigga, you are always going to be my baby brother. All of us in here are ready to go to war for you, Klayton, and no thanks are necessary. How do you want to proceed because at the end of the day, this is your operation now?" Trayce reassured me.

I had let him take the lead because he had the information, and I wanted to hear what he had to say before coming to any conclusions. I didn't want Trayce to put himself at risk going on that date because what if it was a set up? However, we didn't have much other information other than to go after Kamar's family. And if we did that, we would leave all of the women here vulnerable to attack.

"For now, let's keep the plan for the date for tomorrow night. 'am going to need to think before I green light us going forward on this plan tomorrow. The meeting is now adjourned, but I have some news for you guys," I announced, and they all looked at me expectantly.

"What nigga? Some of us want to go lay up in some pussy." Trouble had us all laughing. I could relate because my dick was getting hard thinking of Treasure's wet love box.

"Treasure and I got married in Vegas last week! It was a last-minute decision, but it was one of the best decisions that I made in my life. Once I hit that shit, I knew I had to lock it down so no other nigga could have it. Now the only way out of this marriage for her is death and if she doesn't want another nigga's body on her hand, she better not entertain any other nigga," I announced.

Trayce walked up to me and gave me a hug. "You joined the married club, man? Treasure's young ass got your ass strung out like a crackhead that needs his next hit. It is good to see you happy and in love because you have been through a lot. I'm proud of you."

My relationship with Trayce has always been complicated, to say the least. Ever since I could remember, he was more like a father figure to me than a big brother, then I ended up sleeping with Charlotte. I honestly think that is the reason that made it easier for Trayce to forgive me for what I did to him in the past. I am grateful that he has forgiven me, and our relationship is better than ever now. That was another reason I was on Treasure tough about mending fences with Luca.

"That means a lot to me, bruh. You know I can't apologize enough for how my actions hurt you in the past," I stated sincerely. I really wish I could go back and change how I betrayed my brother, but then I wouldn't be the man that I was today.

"The past is the past. I just want you to know I love your ass, and I'm proud of you."

"KLAYTON, can we go to Dunkin Donuts on the way back? Then I'ma go *bang, bang* nigga and beat your ass in Grand Theft Auto," Little Jah bragged. I ended up bringing Jah to stay the night. He reminded me a lot of myself when I was his age.

"Man, only if I get to beat your ass in NBA 2k and Madden. I am claiming the Lakers and the 49ers as my teams. I'ma fuck some shit up on these damn video games," I bragged.

"Word nigga. I'm about to flex on you and whoop your ass with the Warriors anyways. When Klay Thompson goes off for 40, your ass better not be crying," Little Jah bragged, and I pulled up to Dunkin and went in the drive-thru. I got our snacks and drove back to the house where Treasure had dinner prepared. I sent her a text earlier asking her to get the guest room ready for little Jah. I wanted to spend some time with him because I have been too busy for him lately.

"How has school been going, Jah?" I asked him.

"Man, I got an A on my math test. Math is my weakest subject, but this little girl named Sherry sucked my dick at recess since I let her have my candy," Jah bragged, and I shook my head. I really think Jah is even more of a savage than I was at his age.

"Are you exaggerating? You know you don't have to impress me, Jah. I'm rocking with you regardless," I reminded him.

"Naw, man. She had some pop rocks, did that trick and sucked the soul out of my dick. I didn't stick my puck in her crease though, Klayton. I remember what you guys told me the last time we talked."

"Good. You need to be focused on school and not hoes, Jah. Don't ruin your future playing with these hoes that are looking for an easy come up. Bitches love paid niggas and niggas that are savage, and your ass is a target for hoes," I reminded Little Jah. I needed to teach him how the game works. It's crazy because there was an eight-year-old girl on Maury last week getting a damn paternity test. God forbid if little Jah ends up in that position because my ass would end up catching a body.

"I gotchu. I told Sherry to suck Deez nuts." Little Jah grabbed himself and I almost crashed the fucking car. This little boy was bad as fuck.

“Nigga, your ass gon’ end up with the fucking package if you don’t watch where your ass sticks your dick,” I warned him.

I needed to talk to Derek soon and see if he ever had the birds and the bees talk with Jah. The rest of the drive home was spent with Jah rapping and I was deep in thought about Kamar and making sure Jah was headed down the right path.

30

BRII

That family session I had last week with Nikki and Kobe was eye-opening in a lot of ways. I didn't realize how much I hurt them with the choices that I made, and I was ready to make amends, but I wasn't sure how to. It felt good to know that Kobe didn't hate me, but Nikki really wasn't fucking with me on any level. I had been getting closer to Adrian, and we were sitting outside enjoying the day since it wasn't too cold outside.

"Brii, you have to focus on getting right for yourself. You can't focus on the fact Nikki dislikes you because no matter what she says, Jonah killing himself was not your fault. You made a bad decision when you took those pills, but Jonah's death isn't your fault." Adrian meant well but he had no idea what it was like to deal with the guilt that I was feeling. I also felt bad because the kids are the ones that are suffering the most behind what happened, and if Jonah wasn't here to raise them with me, I simply didn't want to be a part of their lives. It was embarrassing to admit, but I knew they were better off in the care of Nikki and Kobe.

"I do want to get well, Adrian. I'm coming to terms that I'm going to be here for a while. I have a lot of work to do, but I came to terms with a decision that I made," I admitted.

"What decision was that?" Adrian and I were sitting on a blanket outside, and he had poured me a glass of ice-cold lemonade. Adrian had earned a reward because his sessions have been going very well, and he chose to invite me out on a picnic lunch outside. I had to admit the change of scenery was much needed.

"I am signing my rights away for Antoinette, Blake, and Leslie. They deserve much better than I can give them, and they are in good hands," I admitted. I prayed that Adrian wouldn't judge me.

Adrian grabbed my hand and caressed it. I felt butterflies in the pit of my stomach. I was having a hard time fighting my attraction for Adrian. "I care about you a lot, Brii, but I disagree. Children are not like toys that you can throw away when you don't want them—"

I quickly yanked my hand away from him. "Really, Adrian? You act like I asked to be put in a situation where I was stuck raising my siblings. My entire life was a struggle and for once, I just want to be childfree. I love Leslie like he is mine, but I cannot save the world when things are not right in my world. If I'm not good, how can I raise three kids on my own?"

"Brii, check your damn attitude. I know that life was hard, but you are not the only one that grew up with a crackhead mother. There are many people out there raising kids on their own everyday, and I'm sure they struggle, but those kids are their motivation. Jonah would want you to do what is right and make sure those kids are good, and you know it. Hell, I will be here to help you if you will have me," Adrian whispered softly.

"Why do you care, Adrian? In a few days, you will get to go home and go on with your life. You will forget all about me and—"

Adrian put a finger to my lips quieting me. "Brii, I will always be here for you. I will come up here for visiting hours as often as I am allowed. I am falling in love with you. I want to explore a relationship with you when you get out of here, but I also don't want to be a distraction in your life. I will help you raise those kids and make sure you are able to have time for yourself. You have to get out of here and get your life together for the sake of those kids. They didn't ask to be here. You are transmitting your abandonment issues onto them and that is not fair. At one point and time, you were willing to step up to the plate and be there for those kids. You cannot be like every other adult that failed them in their lives and abandon them, Brii. Once you made that commitment to be that mother figure that they needed, you made a life-long commitment. Don't bail on them, Brinisha. I'm begging you not to," Adrian pleaded.

I was in a really selfish place in my life lately. I knew it was unfair to the kids to have to make another transition and adjustment in their lives, but I was convinced that I was no good for them.

"I'm fighting the feelings I have for you, Adrian. When I get out of here, I want to completely forget about the life that I used to live and start over. I need a fresh start and those kids will only be a reminder of Jonah being gone. I simply can't do it, and the more I think about it, the more I admire Treasure and her strength." I had told Adrian all about Treasure's story the other night and wished I was more like her. Even though she wasn't raising Genesis on her own yet, she was actively involved in Genesis life.

"All I hear right now is *I, I, I*. What about what those kids want? When do they get a choice or a say in what goes on in their lives? You won't be taking over care of them tomorrow, Brii because you are still going to be here for a while. All I want is a promise that you will at least consider taking them when you get on your feet. It won't be anytime right now, but those kids deserve a real shot of stability." Adrian was trying to reason with me. I was hearing him, but I didn't completely agree with him. The guilt of how my actions led to this point was keeping me from being able to fully love them like they deserved.

"They do deserve stability, Adrian. I don't know if that is something, I can give them."

"Is that something you can give them, or you are not willing to give them, Brii?" Adrian challenged me with fire in his eyes.

"Hell, if you want me to be honest with you, it is both of those! They deserve much better than what I have to give them emotionally, and I'm not willing to sacrifice my life for them anymore. It is time for me to live for myself instead of living for everyone else. I didn't spread my legs and have those children. I did my best, Adrian. I have lost every fucking thing, and I feel like I am on the verge of a mental breakdown. So, how would I be capable of taking care of three children on my own?" I raged. I hated that I was ruining this picnic with my temper tantrum, but I was also tired of doing what everyone else thought I should do. At the end of the day, I had to live with the consequences of how my life turned out.

"You are really trifling right now, Brii. You are willing to pawn your brother and sister off on other people? I'm disappointed in you, but I have hope you will eventually come around. I know that you are still in treatment and right now just the thought of raising them might be overwhelming for you—"

"Adrian, I need you to listen to me. They are in a good place with Nikki and Kobe. By the time I finish treatment and get myself together, they will be used to staying over there. I love them, but I also have to think about how uprooting them again will affect them. Then, if we end up together, they would have to get to know you and get used to you being in their lives. That is a lot to ask from them." Granted, a lot of my reasoning was selfish, but not all of it was.

"That is why we would take things slowly and go at a pace you and the kids are comfortable with. I'm not saying any of this would be done overnight, but I want you to know this is what we are working towards. I also know that you still love Jonah, and that is another reason I am not rushing you. I know that you are not ready for another relationship right now. It is too soon, but I am in love with you, and I do want to build with you. I don't expect you to say I love you back, but I want you to understand how I feel about you, Brii." Adrian caressed my hand and it felt good. I felt loved. This was a feeling that I'd missed because the last year of my marriage was turbulent.

Were things going too fast between Adrian and me? I don't know, but I do know that I loved this feeling of knowing that someone loved me, and I didn't want to let this go. "I also told Nikki and Kobe during family session that I would sign over custody to them. Nikki wants to file for full custody, and I want to save them the aggravation of going to court because that is the last thing that they need. Nikki and Kobe love them the same way they love their own child, and that is honestly the best place for them," I admitted.

Adrian stared at me intently for a minute before he put his lemonade cup down. "Listen, Brii. If you honestly feel like having Nikki and Kobe take full legal custody of the kids is the best thing for them, I support your decision. I just want you to be sure because that is not something you can change your mind about."

I felt a sense of peace about the decision I was making. I was too selfish minded to raise these kids on my own, and they deserved the stability that Nikki and Kobe could give them. "I have been thinking about this since I had been in session with them. This is the best thing for them, Adrian. I also understand if you change your mind about pursuing me because I do come with a lot of baggage. I also am not ready for anything right now because I still need to grieve and sort through my feelings about Jonah."

Adrian cupped my face in his hands and stared into my eyes. "Brii, you are worth the wait. I will wait as long as I have to. I just want you to get right for yourself and to put in the hard work here. The therapists are here to help you, not hurt you."

"I know. I'm not used to having to be so open and vulnerable with complete strangers. Sometimes when I go to sessions, I feel like I'm being judged, and that is the hardest thing for me to overcome."

There is a big stigma about mental health in the African-American community and I have to admit that I bought into some of the stereotypes about it. I was slowly but surely learning that they were here to help me, but it still wasn't easy for me to accept help.

"You are doing an amazing job, Brii. You have no idea what a remarkable woman you are, and you are stronger than you give yourself credit for. May I kiss you?" Adrian stared deeper into my eyes. He took my breath away.

Was I ready for this? Part of me felt like it was too soon, but I really wanted to feel loved again and be touched and kissed intimately like Jonah used to do. "Yes." That was all I could say and then Adrian kissed me.

It felt like fireworks were going off and I could feel my lady parts getting wet. I wanted to ride Adrian's face and his dick one good time. I was enjoying the kiss, but little did I know, I had an unexpected visitor in a wheelchair. And if I had been paying attention, I would have noticed that it was someone I never would expect. I also didn't notice Nikki and Kobe both looking on in disgust.

31

TREASURE

It was the next day, and I had Little Jah and Genesis with me at the mall. I decided to give my mom a break and take Genesis shopping. I promised Jah I would take his ass to Gamestop for some games before dropping him back off to Derek's house. I wanted to help out and make sure that I would be Klayton's peace and his rock. Klayton was out following up on a lead about Kamar, so I agreed to take the kids off of his hands. Genesis has been confused and calling me and Hope mommy, which was understandable. My mom was the one that raised her, but it was now time for me to step up to the plate and take over care of my daughter. My mom and I agreed we would ease the transition slowly until we all agreed Genesis was ready to move in with Klayton and me. I wanted to do whatever would make this easier on my daughter because that was the priority. I love my parents for being there when I was not in a place where I could take care of Genesis.

"Look, Treasure, that hoe has a fat ass. Can I eat her booty like groceries?" Little Jah asked, and I was tempted to slap the taste out of his mouth. We had just walked in Macy's, and I wanted to look at some outfits. Klayton had given me his black card, and I planned to make a dent in his spending limit.

"Jahquel, I will beat your little ass. My daughter is with me, so watch your mouth!" I warned his ass.

For some reason, Little Jah reminds me of Klayton. His eyes looked kind of like Klayton's, but he really didn't have many facial features of him, so I shook it off. At first, I thought, maybe one of his brothers had an illegitimate child out there somewhere, but I shook that idea off.

"Ain't nothing little about me, including this dick!" Little Jah grabbed himself and I quickly choked his badass up against the wall. He needed an ass whooping, and I was about to give it to him. Unfortunately, I wasn't focused on Genesis and didn't even notice my daughter was missing. I took off my shoe and started whooping Jah's ass in the store, and he stood there taking his spanking like a man.

I finally got tired and stopped to see where Genesis was. "Genesis, where are you?"

"Treasure, her cane is right there, but she is gone," Jahquel pointed out, and I knew then my worst nightmare came true. Someone snatched my daughter up, and I had no idea how to react.

"Genesis, where are you?" I cried hysterically, and I could feel myself start to lose control. I felt Little Jah try to comfort me, and I could tell he felt bad, but this wasn't his fault.

"Hey, lady, bring Genesis back!" Little Jah yelled and took off running. I immediately got myself together when I noticed Little Jah had found Genesis and that little boy was fast as hell. I grabbed my phone and yelled at Siri to call Klayton.

"Yo', what's up, Treasure?" Klayton sounded concerned.

"Some bitch kidnapped Genesis while we were at the mall!" I yelled hysterically.

"Which mall are you guys at? Treasure, I need you to calm down, so I can understand what you are saying!" Klayton yelled.

"I am at the Macy's in the Lakewood Center mall. Nigga hurry up!" I screamed and hung up the phone on his ass. I finally caught up to Little Jah, and he had jumped on that bitch Sparkle's back. This fatal attraction hoe was going to have to fucking go. Why did she come for my ass and why would she not get the hint that Klayton doesn't want her?

Jah poked Sparkle in the eye, and she started screaming. "Demon seed! You fucking little demon seed!"

"Fuck you, hoe! Where the fuck did you think you were taking my daughter? Are you that thirsty for some dick bitch?" I yelled and pulled Jah off of her back. "Jah, go make sure Genesis is ok. I need to beat this bitch ass!"

"I'm taking Danielle away from Klayton, hoe! You are unfit just like I thought when you shot at his daughter. Why won't you admit that you were trying to kill her? Klayton, Danielle and I can be a happy family—" Those were the only words that she got out before I started beating her ass like she stole money.

"I am not unfit! I took my eyes off of Genesis to discipline Jah for one second and that could have happened to any parent. Klayton told you he didn't want your ass and I don't understand why you won't take no for an answer. Klayton isn't attracted to women that look like fucking tires!"

I punched her in the face. She tried grabbing my hair, but I was like a woman possessed. It was one thing if you came for me, but the second you came for my daughter, it was fucking war. Genesis was crying in the background, and I could feel myself start to black out into a rage. I was about to kill this bitch and go to jail when I felt a familiar pair of strong arms pull me off of Sparkle.

"Bae, calm down. You almost killed this bitch in broad daylight. Luckily, I know the police officers that are here and got their ass on the fucking payroll, so they are looking the other way," Klayton whispered.

"Klayton, she has to fucking die. I am sick of this bitch!" I got in one more kick for good measure.

"I'm going to handle Sparkle. We can't do it now because shit is too hot for us to handle it now. Besides, that bitch is about to end up in the hospital with the way you beat her ass. It looks like you broke her ribs and some shit. I can get someone to handle her while she is in the hospital," Klayton whispered.

"Let me go, bae. I need to go check on Genesis and make sure she is ok. By the way, I want her ass arrested for kidnapping." I kissed Klayton on the lips and went to check on the kids.

"Genesis, Mommy is here. Jahquel, you did a great job, and I am proud of you."

"I'm sorry it was my fault the mean lady almost kidnapped Genesis. I won't be bad anymore." Little Jah looked sad.

"Mommy, I love you. Can I have a happy meal?" Genesis asked and tears spilled down my face.

"You can have all the happy meals you want, baby girl. Jah, this wasn't your fault, and I don't want you blaming yourself. You did an amazing job catching Sparkle because she could have gotten away with Genesis. I am so proud of you, Jah, and thank you for helping save my daughter." I hugged both Jah and Genesis and didn't want to let go. Little Jah was trying to get out of my embrace, but my ass wasn't letting his badass go. He is bad, but he has a good heart, just like my husband, Klayton.

An hour later...

Jah and Klayton were ok with Mcdonald's since that was what Genesis wanted. My daughter could ask for the moon right now, and I would try to give it to her. We went to the Mcdonald's inside the Chevron station right outside of the mall and were almost done with our meal.

"Little nigga, get out of my fries, man. You greedy as fuck!" Klayton complained. Genesis and I were laughing at Jah and Klayton fight over their damn fries.

"My fries are all gone, and I want some more." Jah grinned.

"Here you go, Jah, you can have my fries." I gave him what was left of my fries, and Klayton looked at me like I was crazy. I loved how it felt like we were a family and all we really needed was Danielle, who was still at Trayce's house.

"You were about to kill me for stealing your fries, but Jah can have some of your fries? Come on, Treasure," Klayton complained.

"You can have some of my fries, Klayton." Genesis held out her small bag of fries from her happy meal.

"See, someone at this table loves me," Klayton joked and he snatched one of Genesis' french fries.

We didn't get any shopping done but my mood was shot on shopping after what happened with Sparkle. It turns out that police have her under arrest, and she will be going straight to jail on kidnapping charges after she gets out of the hospital. I really didn't feel bad for her. I prayed she got fired because anyone that could kidnap a child should not be working for CPS.

"Jah deserves my fries. He helped saved the day." I took another bite of my Big Mac, but my appetite was ruined. I really couldn't stomach the idea of eating when my daughter almost went missing on my watch. I felt like what happened was my fault even though I knew it wasn't. I felt Klayton squeeze my hand.

"Bae, it wasn't your fault," Klayton whispered.

The kids weren't paying attention because they went back to eating their food, and Genesis had started playing with her happy meal toy. I was trying to hold tears back because Klayton really is my lover and my best friend. He knows me better than I know my damn self. I shouldn't have been surprised that he knew that I was blaming myself.

"I should have kept a better eye on both of them. I was busy reprimanding Jah and—"

"Sshhh. You did what any other parent in that situation would have. You didn't neglect Genesis or do anything that caused her to get hurt. Don't be so hard on yourself. Soon, that bitch Sparkle is going to die, trust me." Klayton held my chin up to meet his. Klayton really is my Superman, so I knew everything he was saying was all facts. Sparkle just signed her damn death certificate.

"I love Genesis so much, and I would have died if anything had happened to her," I whispered.

"Nothing happened to her and Little Jah caught that hoe. I'm definitely going to look out for his ass, but even if Sparkle hadn't gotten away, there would have been nowhere she could hide from my ass. I would have gotten Genesis back." I knew Klayton was right, but I was grateful that it didn't come down to that.

"Are you sure you never fucked her? She is a little too crazy to not at least sample the dick," I whispered, and Klayton grinned.

"Naw, she didn't even get to see my monsta. I knew the day I met her at the hospital that she was playing the good girl role to the max, and she was thirsty for all of this. She never had a chance at getting it though." Klayton winked and I blushed. I might not be hungry for food, but I could definitely go for Klayton going balls deep inside of me later on.

I looked over and saw the kids had finally finished their food. "Let's go home so I can take care of that monsta," I whispered.

Klayton jumped up and grabbed the trash to empty it. I knew better than to even think about trying it. The one time I tried to take the trash out at Klayton's house, he yelled at me so bad, I didn't talk to his ass for twenty-four hours. There were certain things he didn't want me to even think about doing and if he was gone, he would have one of his brothers or someone come by to check on me. If you ask me, it wasn't that deep, but I knew better than to challenge Klayton's crazy ass.

"Genesis, Jah, let's go!" I announced and helped Genesis up. I gave her the cane and held her other hand to help her out of the restaurant.

We started walking towards the car. I was strapping Genesis in Klayton's car when gunshots started going off.

Pow! Pow! Tata! Tata! Blocka! Blocka!

Genesis started crying, and I covered her ears. I heard Klayton pull his gun out and start busting back at whoever was shooting at us.

"Jahquel, get in the car!" Klayton yelled, but it was too late.

Little Jah's body laid there, and it was heartbreaking to watch. He was shot in the stomach.

32

KLAYTON

I was sitting in the emergency room on pins and needles because Little Jah had been in surgery for a while. I had Trayce take Genesis to their house because I felt helpless about keeping her safe. As a man, I felt like I couldn't protect my family and that was the worst feeling in the world. Derek and Jimmya were sitting next to me as well as Trouble and his wife, Veronica. Hope and Giovanni had come for added support, and Nikki was at Ro's house helping her with all of the kids.

"Yo', I am so sorry. I failed Jah and you guys. I never should have been hanging out with him while I had niggas coming for me," I apologized to Derek who was holding a crying Jimmya.

"Naw, man, this wasn't even your fault. I refuse to let you blame yourself for something you couldn't control, man," Derek gave me dap.

Trayce walked in the room interrupting us and walked up to me. "So, I went to go visit Charlotte like I had planned. She was acting funny, and I realized she was on some set up shit. I got out of there because I didn't know what type of time she was on."

"Yo', why did you go alone? That shit could have been a fucking set up, and I could have ended up burying your ass man! You were just supposed to take Genesis to your spot!" I couldn't lose anyone else that I loved, and it was bad enough that no one knew if little Jah was going to make it. An hour ago, the doctor told us that little Jah was going to need a blood transfusion and we all volunteered to give blood. The problem was Derek isn't Jah's biological father. He was already determined to not be a match, so we had to pray that one of us turned out to be a match.

Hope was in the corner of the room praying, and I felt Giovanni walk up to me and give me a hug. "Everything is going to be ok. It's going to work itself out, son."

"If Little Jah doesn't make it. I will never forgive myself."

"I fucking hate you, Klayton! It is your fault Jah is lying there in the back and might die!" Jimmya yelled and her words hurt. I was blaming myself for what happened, but it hurt to know that she felt that way. I wasn't Jimmya's favorite person lately because she felt like I encouraged Little Jah's bad behavior.

"Jimmya, chill out!" Derek ordered, and she punched him in the chest.

"Fuck you, Derek. You and Klayton teaching that boy to act like a street nigga," Jimmya complained and then stomped off towards the bathroom.

Kobe had just gotten here, and it looked like he was pushing someone in a wheelchair. I was confused because I had no idea who the fuck that could have been. "Kobe, who the hell is that?"

"Man, I'm here to get my blood tested for Little Jah and Jonah wants to donate blood," Kobe announced. He turned the wheelchair around and that was Jonah's ass. I could have sworn the nigga was fucking dead.

"Yo', what in the entire fuck? Are we going to give little Jah ghost blood?" I yelled and the color left my face. Hell, Jonah shot himself in the head, so how the hell was he even alive? I had so many questions, but now was not the time to get answers.

"Klayton, I promise you I will explain when shit calms down but for now, let me and Jonah go get tested to see if we are a match." Kobe hugged me then went to the front desk.

A few minutes later, a nurse summoned Kobe, who wheeled Jonah to the back. I was so shocked, I didn't even get to say anything to the nigga, but I was grateful that he was alive and well. Hopefully, Jonah and Brii would make their marriage work now that they were both ok.

"I should have taken them straight home from the mall, man. What if that Sparkle bitch was working with Kamar? It seems too coincidental that Sparkle tries to kidnap Genesis earlier and then we get shot at leaving Mcdonalds." I was talking to myself, but Giovanni was listening.

"Yo', what the fuck?" Giovanni yelled.

"Genesis is fine and she's is at Trayce's house now. Little Jah found the crazy bitch that kidnapped Genesis, and Treasure beat her damn ass. She is in the hospital and under arrest now for kidnapping."

"You should have called me as soon as something was up. You know that I would have dropped everything to come to help you, man." Giovanni looked pissed, and I couldn't blame him.

"Man, I wasn't thinking at the time, Giovanni. The second Treasure called me, I was trying to get to her as soon as possible. I know that I should have called you, and I apologize but I wasn't thinking straight," I explained. I knew damn well I would have been pissed if I was in Giovanni's shoes.

"First, Jonah's ass comes back from the dead, who knows where that nigga has been hiding out at. Now I find out my granddaughter was kidnapped, and we don't even know who the hell kidnapped her. On God, bodies are about to start flying," Giovanni ranted, and I agreed with him on all of this. I knew that we were going to have to make a trip to Philly and make Kamar and the people associated with this fuck nigga pay.

"There is so much going on but trust me, I never would have put Treasure or Genesis in harm's way. I definitely wouldn't have had Jah in harm's way, and I am trying to figure out now if Sparkle is somehow connected to Kamar."

Trayce walked up and joined the conversation. "Yo' I got the PI looking up the Sparkle bitch and if there is a connection there, you know the PI will find it. I'm also having him find her information on where her parents live or other relatives. The second she involved Genesis is the second her family became fair game. I'm also getting ready to let Trouble and Derek head to Philly."

"Good looking, man. We shouldn't say too much here, but I'm with it. This Kamar nigga is determined to break my ass down."

Trayce looked at me. "We aren't going to let it happen. I know you are feeling weak right now, but Kobe and I are here for you. Trust me, I'm getting ready for war because I'm ready to go on an old-fashioned killing spree just like I used to back in the day. I need you to hold it together because Treasure needs you to be strong. If you go out there weak then you leave yourself vulnerable to get bodied."

"I feel you, man. I wish it was me back there on that table and not little Jah. I wish I could trade places with him. And to hear Genesis cry earlier when those gunshots went off broke my heart. Maybe I should leave Treasure since I'm no good for her. All I keep doing is put her in positions where her life is in danger. She has a child that she needs to live for and—"

"I'm pissed right now, but you are not going to take the cowards way out and leave my daughter. You guys need each other and remember, you have an entire team ready to go to war with you, son. I don't call you *son* lightly. You really are like a son to me, Klayton." Giovanni stared at me intently and I could hear the sincerity in his words. It meant a lot to me knowing that he considered me a son because I never had a real father. Trayce was like a father to me in a sense, but he was only supposed to be my big brother.

"I know how you feel, bruh, because you have been put in positions—" Trayce was interrupted by Kobe wheeling Jonah out, and they had a sad look on their face.

"Man, neither of us are a match, bro, but I heard that the doctor might be coming out with some news in a minute man. Let's pray." Kobe looked devastated. He didn't even know Little Jah like that, but I do know that he would never wish anything like this to happen to a kid.

"Yo' Jonah, it is good to see you, man. Where the hell have you been hiding and how are you feeling?" I asked, concerned about his condition. I couldn't bare to talk about the situation with little Jah right now.

"Man, I'm in the land of the living. I tried taking myself out after what happened with Brii, but it wasn't my time. Kobe has been keeping me up to date on her condition but at this point, I'm on some fuck that bitch kind of time," Jonah said bitterly. I was confused. I thought he would have been happy about Brii being alive, but I was missing something.

"I thought you would have been happy to know about Brii—"

"Naw, that bitch is a whore real talk. She is a mental health clinic moving on with the next nigga, I mean bitch. I saw it with my own eyes. Kobe and Nikki took me down to visit Brii, and we were going to surprise her. I saw her having a picnic with this hoe named Adrian. Hell, I would have thought that Brii would have at least let my remains settle in the ground before trying to move on."

"Are you sure you didn't misinterpret it? That doesn't even sound like the Brii we all know."

"Man, I'm with Jonah. Fuck that hoe. I took Jonah down there, and we were going to tell Brii that Jonah is alive, but we saw her and Adrian making out and looking cozy over a picnic lunch. Nikki was right about that bitch, she didn't deserve the benefit of the doubt. I was feeling sorry for the bitch too." Kobe shook his head.

There was so much drama going on, and I was sick at the thought of it. There was no way to dispute the fact that she was making out with another man, especially if Kobe and Jonah both saw it. "

Did you guys confront her?"

"Hell naw, I would have caught a fucking case. When I get better, I'm going to get custody of the kids and divorce Brii's hoe ass. I deserve better than what she gave me. The joke is on her though." Jonah paused and then continued. "I had that Adrian nigga investigated, and it turns out he is really a she. Adrian is a fucking female, so they must not have had sex yet." Jonah had a sinister grin on his face.

"What the fuck?" I asked.

"Adrian had gender reassignment surgery two years ago, but I doubt Adrian was real enough to admit it. I wonder how Brii would feel if she really knew the truth—"

"Klayton Jackson?" Dr. Whitfield, the doctor from earlier, announced. I got up to meet the doctor. Everyone immediately followed and Kobe pushed Jonah's wheelchair.

"What's up, doc?" I asked, praying that I would be a match and could give blood. The doctor had a grin on his face, so I assumed the doctor found someone that would be a match.

"The good news is we found a match for Little Jah, and you are a perfect match," Dr. Whitfield beamed, and I was excited.

"That is wonderful news! Where do I go to give blood?" I asked eagerly.

"I will take you to the back to get that started immediately because time is of the essence. You know what this means, right?" Dr. Whitfield asked.

"No. What does that mean?"

"You, Klayton Jackson, are the biological father of Jahquel Marino."

Oh, you thought we were done?????? Part 4 is in the works!!!!!!!!
Do you guys feel bad for Brii or did she move on from Jonah too quickly?

COMING NEXT!

CPSIA information can be obtained
at www.ICGtesting.com
Printed in the USA
LVHW091815230819
628744LV00003B/454/P